CAMP SUNNYSIDE FRIENDS #17

Camp Spaghetti

Marilyn Kaye

AN AVON CAMELOT BOOK

CAMP SUNNYSIDE FRIENDS #17: CAMP SPAGHETTI is an original publication of Avon Books. This work has never before appeared in book form.

AVON BOOKS
A division of
The Hearst Corporation
1350 Avenue of the Americas
New York, New York 10019

Copyright © 1992 by Marilyn Kaye
Published by arrangement with the author
Library of Congress Catalog Card Number: 91-93037
ISBN: 0-380-76556-X
RL: 4.9

First Avon Camelot Printing: April 1992

CAMELOT TRADEMARK REG. U.S. PAT OFF. AND IN OTHER COUNTRIES, MARCA REGISTRADA, HECHO EN U.S.A.

Printed in the U.S.A.

OPM 10 9 8 7 6 5 4 3 2 1

For Marie-Hèléne Polloni and Vincent Souleil

Camp Spaghetti

Chapter 1

Erin Chapman stood in front of the mirror in the locker room at Miss Harrington's School for Girls. As she pulled a brush through her long, blonde hair, she tried to form her lips into a smile. Usually, that wasn't difficult, because most of the time she was pleased with her appearance. But today, she was feeling a little low, and it wasn't easy stretching her lips.

She tried to think of something that would make her feel more cheerful. There was only one class left before school let out for the day— that was nice. And in just two weeks, she'd be having the last gym class for ten days. Spring break was just around the corner.

She concentrated on looking forward to that. For ten glorious days, there would be no volleyball, no homework, no pop quizzes. As she adjusted the collar of her shirt, she remembered

1

something else—she wouldn't have to wear this awful uniform for ten days either.

Looking ahead like that made her smile. Then, another figure joined her at the mirror. "Hi, Erin."

Erin's smile faded. "Hello, Carla," she replied coolly.

In the mirror, she concentrated on applying mascara, but out of the corner of her eye she watched as Carla carefully outlined her mouth with a lip pencil. At least while Carla was doing that, she couldn't talk.

But as soon as Carla finished coloring her lips, she spoke again.

"Do you have any special plans for spring break?"

Erin made an *mmm* sound that didn't say yes or no. Luckily, at that moment, two of her friends joined them at the mirror.

"I hate volleyball," Marcia announced.

Hilary, who was always optimistic, piped up. "But just think, in two weeks we'll be free!"

"Only for ten days," Marcia muttered.

"Oh well, it's better than ten days here!" Hilary said cheerfully.

Carla turned to them. "Have you guys got any particular plans for spring break?"

"Nothing special," Hilary said. "How about you? What are you doing?"

"Nothing special," Carla repeated. "Of course, as soon as school is out for the summer, I'll be going away with my family. We're visiting Italy this year."

Erin rolled her eyes. Carla was always bragging about her travels. The summer before, she'd gone to France, and the girls had been forced to look at slides and listen to Carla's description of her trip in a special school assembly.

"Actually, I don't mind staying here in town over spring break," Carla continued. "It will be fun having more time to spend with Alan."

Erin saw her friends' eyes turn away from Carla and toward her. And she could feel her own lips tighten. But she refused to let Carla see any reaction. She couldn't think of a good comeback, so she just stayed grimly silent. Still, Carla shot her a triumphant smirk. Then she whirled around and headed back to her locker.

In the mirror, Erin could see the sympathy in her friends' eyes.

"What a creep," Hilary said.

"Don't let her bother you," Marcia added.

Erin tossed her head so her blonde curls bounced on her shoulders. "Don't worry about

3

me," she assured her friends. "Alan's a jerk. I don't know what I saw in him in the first place. As far as I'm concerned, Carla's welcome to him."

"That's the spirit," Hilary stated, and Marcia nodded encouragingly.

Basically, Erin had been honest with her friends. She really didn't miss Alan, even though he'd been her sort-of boyfriend for almost a year. Alan was cute and all that, but he certainly wasn't the boy of her dreams. Sometimes he could be really boring. And he was so immature!

She remembered the last time they'd been together. They'd been at the pizza parlor with a bunch of other kids. Everything was fine, or at least ordinary, until Alan took a straw and blew its wrapper at another boy. That got all the boys started shooting straw wrappers. Then Alan aimed one at *her*—and it hit her right between the eyes.

Of course, it was only a straw wrapper and it didn't hurt. But she knew by the way everyone was laughing that she must have looked silly. The whole scene was seriously infantile.

But even so, she wished *she'd* been the one to end the relationship. Not that there had been any real breakup. Alan didn't have that kind of nerve.

4

What he did was worse. He showed up at the pizza parlor the very next night with Carla. By Monday morning, every girl at her school knew about it. And if there was one thing Erin hated, it was the idea that anyone felt sorry for her. The expressions of sympathy she encountered in the halls made her feel much worse than knowing she wouldn't be hanging out at the pizza parlor with Alan anymore.

No, she really wouldn't miss Alan. Let Carla get straw wrappers blown in her face. Still, she'd miss having someone to call a boyfriend. It was humiliating, being dumped like that. And especially for someone like Carla, who loved reminding Erin that she now had Erin's old boyfriend.

Firmly, she pushed all that out of her mind and turned to her friends. "What *are* we going to do over the spring break?"

"Shop," Hilary replied promptly. "All the summer clothes are in the stores now."

"Sounds good to me," Erin said.

"We can sleep late every day," Marcia added, "and watch all the soap operas."

"That new amusement park is going to open," Erin noted. "We could go to that."

"Sure," Marcia agreed. "And I'm going to have a party."

Both Erin and Hilary looked at her in surprise. "You are?" Hilary asked. "What's the occasion? It's not your birthday."

"My cousin's coming to visit," Marcia explained.

Erin's eyebrows shot up. "Which cousin?"

"Charles. You remember him. He visited last year."

Erin's mouth fell open. But before any words could come out, there was the sound of a shrill whistle. Then the gym teacher clapped her hands twice.

"All right, girls, line up and return to your classroom."

With the teacher marching directly behind her, Erin didn't dare speak to Marcia in the hallway. Once they were back in class, their regular teacher, Miss Booth, announced that they'd spend the last hour of the day reading silently. As the girls pulled out their library books, Miss Booth sat at her desk and gazed at them all keenly. There would be no chance for Erin to pass a note to Marcia.

Her head was spinning. She propped an open book on her desk, but it could have been upside down for all she knew or cared.

She certainly did remember Marcia's cousin. And what she remembered was very pleasant.

Charles was a *doll*, a major hunk. He was great looking, he wore sharp clothes, and he was totally cool. Erin had been awed when she'd met him briefly at Marcia's a year ago.

Back then, Charles had been polite, but he hadn't paid much attention to Erin. She couldn't blame him. She'd only been eleven, and he was thirteen. But now, she was twelve. And that could make a big difference.

Funny, to think that just a few minutes earlier she'd been feeling down. Now, her spirits were high. Shopping and sleeping late and watching soap operas were all very nice things to look forward to, but now she had something even better.

She began making plans in her head. First, she'd have to find out when he was due to arrive. Then, about an hour or so later, she'd drop by Marcia's, very casually. She'd need an excuse so this wouldn't look obvious to Charles. She must have a sweater or something at home that she'd borrowed from Marcia.

Charles might not remember that they'd met before, but so what? He'd take one look at the much-more-mature, sophisticated Erin, and—

"Erin?"

The teacher's voice startled her out of her fantasies. "Yes, Miss Booth?"

"Reading rather slowly, aren't you?"

Erin reddened. Miss Booth's sharp eyes obviously hadn't missed the fact that her book had been open to the same page for at least fifteen minutes. "Sorry. I guess I was daydreaming."

Miss Booth sighed and moved on. Erin tried to concentrate on her book. She was getting as bad as her cabin mate from Camp Sunnyside, Megan Lindsay, who always had her head in the clouds.

But she couldn't help it. Her eyes scanned a couple of lines, and then all she could see was the inside of her closet. What should she wear the first time she saw Charles?

This was so perfect! It was exactly what she needed—a new boyfriend. Someone she could be with and be seen with—particularly by Carla and Alan! Okay, maybe this romance would last only the length of Charles's visit. But then there would be letters she could show off at school.

Finally, the bell rang. Erin found it particularly difficult to follow the standard procedure—to rise, stay by her desk until Miss Booth dismissed the class, and then file out in an orderly fashion.

The minute she was out of the building, she clutched Marcia's arm. "Tell me, when is he coming?"

"Who?" Marcia asked, her face all innocence. Then she grinned. She knew Erin very well. "Oh, Charles. I'll find out when my aunt calls my mother today."

Hilary giggled. "I can't imagine why you're so interested, Erin."

"Let's go to the Soda Shoppe," Erin said happily. "My treat."

"Your treat?" Marcia asked. "How come?"

Erin laughed. "It's a bribe. So you'll tell me *everything* about your cousin."

By the time Erin arrived home an hour later, she had a complete file on Charles in her head. Marcia had seen him at Christmas, and she assured Erin he was still cute. He was playing football now, he was president of his class, and as far as Marcia knew, he didn't have a steady girlfriend. Erin couldn't have picked a more perfect guy if she'd created him herself.

"Hello, Nora," she sang out as she entered the foyer of her large house.

The housekeeper seemed a bit taken aback with her warm greeting, and Erin couldn't blame her. She'd been wearing a long face the last few days.

"Hello, Erin. Your mother just called. She's shopping, and she's meeting your father at the

9

office. They'll be coming home together in time for dinner."

Privately, Erin was glad her mother wasn't home. She wanted time alone to fantasize and plan and work out her wardrobe for the entire spring break.

Once in her room, she quickly took off her school uniform and slipped into some jeans. Passing the mirror, she gave herself a once-over. Surely, no one would take her for just twelve. She definitely looked at least thirteen. And that was certainly old enough for a fourteen-year-old boy.

Her eyes fell on a framed snapshot, sitting on her dresser. What was *that* still doing there? Quickly, she opened the back of the frame and pulled out the photo of Alan. She tore it into little pieces and dropped them in the wastebasket. Maybe she'd be replacing it with a much better-looking photo soon.

She noticed that removing the photo had revealed another one which had been under it. She'd forgotten it was there.

It was a picture of her cabin mates, taken at Camp Sunnyside the summer before. She remembered the occasion. They'd been all dressed up, ready to go to a social over at Camp Eagle across the lake. Their counselor, Carolyn, had taken the picture.

She studied it for a moment. There was little red-haired Megan, the daydreamer. And Katie, looking as uncomfortable as she always did in a dress. Sarah was turned slightly to the side— she always did that when she posed for pictures, because she thought it made her look slimmer. Tall, slender Trina was smiling shyly.

It was odd to think that Trina and Sarah were sisters now. Of course, they wouldn't look alike since they weren't blood sisters. Trina's mother had married Sarah's father, just a couple of months ago. Erin had gone to the wedding, and so had Katie and Megan.

They were all good friends, though Erin had always considered herself to be much more mature. Briefly, she wondered if any of them had found a boyfriend in the last two months. She doubted it. They just weren't ready for real romance.

But Erin was. Just thinking about spring break made her feel giddy with excitement. She scampered over to her huge walk-in closet.

But before she could begin studying her wardrobe, the phone by her bed rang. It was her own private line, so she knew it was for her. She flung herself across her bed and picked it up.

11

"Hello?"

"Hi, Erin, it's Marcia."

"Hi! Did your aunt call? When is Charles coming?"

Marcia's voice was subdued. "He's not."

A cold shiver crept up Erin's spine. "What?"

"He's not coming. His parents are going on a cruise, and he's going with them."

Only seconds before, Erin had felt like she was floating inside a balloon. Now Marcia had pierced that balloon with a pin. Erin could feel herself plummeting to earth.

"He's not coming," she repeated dully.

"Sorry to get your hopes up," Marcia said. "Oh, well, it's no big deal. We can still go to the amusement park, and shop . . ."

Erin didn't even listen as Marcia elaborated on possible activities for spring break. Suddenly, none of those plans sounded like fun at all.

When she finally hung up, Erin remained on the bed. Depression hung over her like a big, gray cloud. All her plans, all her glorious expectations . . . they were gone, completely gone.

If only Marcia hadn't told her about Charles in the first place! Maybe she'd been feeling gloomy before, but now she was utterly miserable.

She had nothing to look forward to. Her fantasies began to turn into horrible predictions. They'd end up doing the same old ordinary things, she and Marcia and Hilary. And everywhere they'd go, they'd run into Carla and Alan. At the mall, the movies, the country club, there they'd be. Each time she'd see them, Carla would shoot Erin one of those triumphant smirks. And other kids would look at Erin in pity, with expressions that read oh you poor pathetic creature, getting dumped like that for Carla.

She couldn't bear it, she just couldn't bear it! She put her head in her hands. But she was too depressed to even cry.

She was still in that position when Nora rapped on her door. "Erin, your parents are home. It's dinnertime."

It took some effort to pull herself off the bed. Listlessly, she dragged herself out of the room, down the stairs, and into the dining room.

Her parents were already at the table. "Hello, dear," her mother said.

"Hi," Erin murmured.

"How was your day?" her father asked.

"Fine."

But from the concerned looks on her parents'

faces, she knew her one-word reply wasn't very convincing.

Her father frowned. "Is something wrong?"

"Are you feeling all right?" her mother asked.

"I'm fine," Erin repeated.

Nora began serving the food. Erin didn't even notice what it was. She picked up her fork and poked at whatever was on her plate.

But she was aware that her parents hadn't taken their eyes off her. That was the problem with being an only child. You got all the attention. Of course, sometimes that worked to your advantage, too. But not tonight.

"Darling, I can tell something is wrong," her mother insisted. "What's bothering you?"

There was no way she could tell them. They wouldn't understand. But she was going to have to give them some kind of an answer, or they'd be questioning her all night.

"I'm just depressed," she said finally.

"About what?" her father asked.

"I don't know," Erin said. "Just ... depressed, that's all."

Now they *really* looked worried. Usually, Erin was very specific about her complaints. And her parents usually responded with some effort to cheer her up—a new dress, a piece of jewelry, a holiday. Her friends were always teasing her about being spoiled. Erin didn't think she was spoiled. She simply had parents who gave her everything she wanted.

But her parents couldn't supply her with a boyfriend. And this time, she couldn't be cheered with a new dress or bracelet or holiday. . . .

She drew in her breath sharply. A holiday. At least she wouldn't have to be here in town, running into Alan and Carla. She raised her eyes. Her parents gazed into them hopefully.

"Mom, Dad . . . could we take a holiday and go somewhere over spring break?"

Sincere regret shone in their eyes. "Sweetheart, it's impossible for me to get away from the office this month," her father said.

"And I'm completely tied up with the garden club exhibition," her mother said.

Erin slumped back into her seat. "Oh. Okay."

"You'll be able to go to the country club every day," her mother offered. "You can play tennis and swim and be with your friends . . ." Her voice trailed off as Erin's expression didn't change.

"I just wanted to get away," Erin murmured.

"Would you like to visit your aunt?" her father asked.

"Or one of your Sunnyside friends?" her mother suggested.

Neither of those ideas sounded too thrilling. Erin shook her head and poked at her food.

But her parents weren't giving up. "Where would you like to go, Erin?" her mother beseeched her.

Vaguely, Erin considered the question. She had no idea. Someplace different, exciting. Someplace that would impress Carla and everyone else. That would be nice, to go someplace where Carla hadn't been yet, so she could show off a little.

Where was it Carla had said she was going next summer? She tried to remember the conversation in the locker room.

She raised her woebegone eyes and presented her parents with a small, wistful smile.

"Italy?"

Chapter 2

Katie Dillon ambled into the kitchen. Her father was loading the dishwasher with dinner plates.

"Any pie left over?" Katie asked him.

Mr. Dillon put a finger to his lips. "Shh, your mother's on the phone."

Katie looked over her shoulder. Sure enough, her mother stood there, with the phone pressed tightly to her ear. She wasn't saying anything, but she was definitely listening. Katie knew her mother's expressions well enough to see that whatever she was listening to, it must be something pretty serious. Mrs. Dillon's forehead was puckered, and she was biting her lip.

Mr. Dillon closed the dishwasher, and glanced at his wife. Silently, she mouthed the word "later." He raised his eyebrows for a second, and then left the room.

Probably one of her college students, calling with a problem, Katie thought. But when her mother finally spoke, she didn't sound like she was addressing a student. Her voice was uncertain.

"I—I don't know what to say. That's quite an offer."

Katie watched her curiously for a second. But whoever was on the other line must have been doing a lot of talking, since her mother fell silent again.

She opened the refrigerator and devoted herself to an examination of the contents. Behind her, she heard her mother speak again.

"Yes, certainly, it does sound like a marvelous opportunity. Of course, I'll have to discuss it with my husband."

Katie couldn't find any pie. Obviously, her twin brothers had beaten her to the refrigerator. Was there anything else worth eating? Halfheartedly, she took an apple. It wasn't what she craved.

But her mother's next words chased all thoughts of food from her mind.

"Thank you very much, Mrs. Chapman. I'll get back to you about this right away."

Katie whirled around. The only Mrs. Chapman she knew was the mother of one of her

18

Sunnyside cabin mates. The only time her mother ever spoke to Mrs. Chapman was when some kind of Sunnyside get-together was being organized. Katie usually planned those activities, but now obviously something she didn't know about was happening.

Mrs. Dillon replaced the phone and gazed at it thoughtfully.

"Was that Erin's mother?" Katie asked eagerly. "What did she want? What's going on?"

Her mother was silent for a few seconds before she spoke. "Katie, I need to talk with your father privately."

Katie began to protest. "But I want to know—"

Her mother didn't let her get any farther. *"Katie.* Get your father." That no-nonsense tone meant the subject wasn't up for discussion.

Katie gave a shrug of defeat and ambled out of the kitchen. She could hear her father down in the basement, talking to her brothers. "Dad," she called down, "Mom wants you."

Then she tore upstairs to the bathroom. She closed the door and knelt on the floor next to the sink.

There was a heating vent there. And Katie knew from experience that anything said in the kitchen could be heard through this vent. As she pressed her ear against it, she heard the scrape of a chair as her father sat down at the kitchen table. Then she heard her mother's voice.

"That was Louise Chapman. You remember Erin Chapman, one of Katie's Sunnyside friends."

"That's the very wealthy one, right?"

"Yes. And her mother just issued the most amazing invitation."

Katie was cramped and uncomfortable, curled up on the floor. But there was no way she'd risk missing a word by shifting her position. She strained to listen as her mother continued.

"It seems they want to send Erin on a cultural trip to Italy over spring break. But they were too late to get her into one of those organized student tours. So Mrs. Chapman's trying to form one. And she wants Katie to go."

Katie clapped a hand over her mouth. She didn't think a gasp could be heard in the kitchen through the vent, but she wasn't taking any chances.

Her father's gasp was completely audible. "Italy!"

"Yes. For ten days. She's inviting all the girls from Katie's cabin at Sunnyside."

There was a silence. Then her father spoke in

a steady, measured voice. "It would be a wonderful opportunity for her. But we can't afford to send Katie to Italy for ten days."

"That's the most incredible part. The Chapmans would cover the expenses for all the girls. The flight, the hotel, meals—everything."

"Are you serious?"

"Well, they *are* very wealthy," Mrs. Dillon reminded him.

"But even so . . . we can't accept such a grand offer."

"That's what I thought at first. Then Mrs. Chapman started going on about how we'd had Erin here for visits, and how we took her skiing last winter."

Mr. Dillon laughed. "I suppose that given our finances compared to theirs, our taking Erin to a ski resort would be like their taking Katie to Italy."

"Actually, they wouldn't be taking the girls themselves," Mrs. Dillon said. "They're sending Carolyn, the girls' counselor from Sunnyside, to act as guide and chaperone."

No more words came through the vent. For a few seconds, Katie was afraid her parents had left the room to continue the conversation. It was a relief when her father's voice came through again.

"It would be a shame to deprive her of an opportunity like this."

"But . . . Italy! It's so far away."

Italy. Katie tried to remember her geography lessons and visualize a map of the world. Just then, there was a banging on the bathroom door.

She covered the vent with her hand. "I'm in here!" she yelled. "Go away!"

"Hurry up!" barked Michael or Peter—even their voices were exactly alike.

Katie removed her hand from the vent and pressed her ear against it again. But she couldn't hear a thing. Say yes, she pleaded silently, please say yes.

Again, she heard banging on the door. "Go away!" she shrieked.

Whichever twin it was responded. "Mom and Dad want you in the kitchen. *Now.*"

Katie leaped up and pulled the door open. She tore past the startled twin and ran down the stairs. She slowed down as she approached the kitchen, and tried to enter casually. "Hi. You want me?"

Her mother gazed at her seriously. "Well?"

Katie stepped back. "Well what?"

"Do you want to go?" her father asked.

Katie attempted a look of wide-eyed innocence. "Go where?"

22

Her father's lips twitched. Her mother smiled broadly. "Honestly, Katie," she said. "Do you think we don't know about the vent in the bathroom?"

At least they didn't look angry, so Katie didn't even try to deny it. "Can I go, Mom? Dad? Can I?"

"Do you *want* to go to Italy?" her father asked.

Katie began hopping up and down. "Of course I do!"

Her mother smiled. "Then it's okay with us."

Katie let out a squeal. The twin walked in and gazed at her in bewilderment. "What's going on?" Peter asked.

Katie began dancing around the room. "I'm going to Italy! I'm going to Italy!" Then, abruptly, she stopped dancing. "Mom, Dad . . ."

They spoke together. "Yes?"

"Where *is* Italy?"

Megan Lindsay pulled the atlas off the shelf in the den and placed the oversized book on the floor. She opened it to the map of the world.

She knew which continent to find—Europe. Then she spotted Italy. It was the country shaped like a boot.

She looked back at the facing page, which

contained North America, and placed a finger on Pennsylvania. Slowly, she traced a path from there to Rome.

Italy was all the way across the Atlantic Ocean. On the two pages, it didn't look so far. But Megan knew how great the distance must be. Once, her whole family had driven to Connecticut. It was only an inch away from Pennsylvania on the map, but the trip had taken hours.

Her mother came in the room. "What are you looking at?"

"Italy. It's so far away! It must take ages to get there from here."

"Not by plane," Mrs. Lindsay assured her. "They go very fast."

Megan almost smiled. Of course, she knew a person couldn't drive over an ocean! "My first plane ride," she murmured.

"It's fun," her mother said. "You won't even know how high up you are."

"Of course I will, if I look out the window."

"You won't be able to see anything," her mother said. "Oh, maybe a few clouds. But you'll be flying at night. As I recall, your flight leaves at seven in the evening, and arrives in Rome at around eight A.M."

"Eight A.M.," Megan repeated. She did some

rapid mental calculations. "That's thirteen hours!"

Her mother laughed. "No, dear, it's only seven hours. The time zone is different, remember?"

Megan gave her an abashed grin. Of course, she knew that. "Oh yeah, it's later in Italy, right? How many hours?"

"I think Italy is six hours ahead of us. When you land in Rome, it will be eight in the morning there. But for us back here, it's only two A.M."

Megan frowned. "I'll be losing a lot of hours."

"You'll get them back on your return," her mother said.

Megan nodded. Still, it was weird thinking that she could be eating lunch while everyone back home was still sleeping. It gave her an odd feeling.

Lunch. That made her think of something else. "Do they eat the same foods in Italy that we eat here?"

"Some foods are the same, but . . ." She paused as Mr. Lindsay entered the room. "Did you get Alex to sleep?"

"He's sleeping like a baby," Megan's father replied. "Which I suppose makes sense, since he *is* a baby. What are you two talking about?"

Mrs. Lindsay grinned. "Three guesses."

"Italy, Italy, Italy," Mr. Lindsay replied.

"Megan wants to know what people eat there."

"Ah." Her father sighed deeply and rolled his eyes in ecstasy. "Only the most wonderful, delicious food in the whole wide world."

"You know, Megan, some of your favorite foods are Italian," her mother pointed out. "Pizza, spaghetti . . ."

"And they have the best ice cream in the universe," her father proclaimed. "The Italians are famous for it!"

Well, that was good news. "Do they have Heath Bar crunch?" Megan asked hopefully.

"I don't know all the flavors," her father said. "But I'm sure you'll find a few you'll enjoy, even if they have different names."

That's right, Megan thought, the names of the flavors will be in Italian. She didn't know any Italian. How would she know which flavor to ask for? What if she picked an ice cream and it turned out to be pistachio? She *hated* pistachio.

"What else is different in Italy?" she asked. "They use different money from ours, right?" She remembered when her grandmother had come back from a trip to France. She'd brought Megan some coins called francs.

Mrs. Lindsay nodded. "The Italian money is called lire."

"Leerah," Megan repeated. It didn't sound like real money to her.

Her father spelled it. "L-I-R-E."

Megan frowned. "Why don't they spell it the way it's pronounced?"

"Because Italian pronunciation is different from English," her mother said.

Megan shivered. Images raced through her mind. Flying over an ocean at night. Clocks that were all wrong, food with strange names, money that wasn't dollars and cents, words that weren't pronounced the way they were spelled.

"I've always wanted to see Rome." Mr. Lindsay sighed. "All those ancient buildings . . ."

"Like in Connecticut?" Megan asked. They'd visited a town there that had a two-hundred-year-old house.

Her father grinned. "A lot older than anything in Connecticut! You'll see ruins that were built in the first century!"

Megan grimaced. Old run-down buildings didn't sound very attractive to her.

"Megan, what's wrong?" her mother asked.

Megan swallowed. "I guess I'm a little nervous. . . ."

Her father tousled her red curls. "You're going to love Italy."

"How do you know?" Megan asked. "You just said you've never been there."

Mrs. Lindsay slipped her arm through her husband's. "We'll go someday."

"Why don't you come with us?" Megan asked quickly.

"I wish we could," her father said. Then his face became serious. "Don't tell me you're going to be homesick!"

Megan shrugged.

"Darling, it's only for ten days," her mother noted. "You go away to Camp Sunnyside every year for the whole summer!"

But that was different, Megan wanted to cry out. Camp Sunnyside was like a second home to her. She knew everything about Sunnyside, it was always familiar, and all her friends were there.

She gave herself a mental shake. All her friends would be in Italy with her. It would be just like Camp Sunnyside—only in a different place. What was she so scared of, anyway?

Her parents were watching her anxiously. Megan grinned. "No, I won't be homesick."

Just then, a wail floated out to the room. Megan jumped up. "I'll get him."

She hurried down the hall to her baby brother's room. Okay, maybe Italy would feel weird and strange and totally unfamiliar. But she'd be with the whole cabin six gang. They'd be sharing all the new experiences and adventures together.

Alex was standing up in his crib, gripping the bars. He stopped crying when he saw Megan and made noises that sounded like "a-gah, a-gah." Megan scooped him up in her arms.

"I'm going to Italy, Alex," she murmured. "And I'll have so much to tell you when I get back."

Too bad he wouldn't understand a word of it!

"Sarah! Trina! Come here for a minute."

With a sigh Sarah replaced the milk she'd just taken out of the refrigerator.

Trina grinned. "I think it's time for another lesson."

Sure enough, when they walked into the den, Dr. Fine was clutching a book. "Listen to this," he said, and began to read. " 'The Roman Forum, or *Foro Romano,* was the political and religious center of ancient Rome. Here you will see a vast array of ruined temples and public buildings. Follow the Via Sacra past the three arches . . .' "

Sarah and Trina exchanged looks and muffled giggles. Ever since they'd found out they were going to Italy for spring break, Sarah's father had been trying to instruct them in Italian history. Sometimes, to Sarah, it seemed like he was more excited about this trip than they were!

His voice droned on. Sarah didn't want to tell him that she and Trina had already read practically everything they could get their hands on about Italy. He was enjoying this too much.

Luckily, just as she was about to fidget, Trina's mother burst into the room. She started laughing.

"Okay, professor, give the class a break!"

Dr. Fine looked up, and pretended to be injured. "I'm not forcing the girls to listen to this. They *want* to learn about Italy. Right, girls?"

"Oh, sure, sure," Sarah said quickly.

"Absolutely," Trina echoed. Then they couldn't help themselves. They started giggling.

Dr. Fine sighed. "I only want them to understand what they see and appreciate it."

Trina's mother nodded. "But they're leaving tomorrow, dear, and they need to start packing. And we need to give them their going-away gifts."

Sarah and Trina leaped up. Dr. Fine closed his book, and went to a bureau. Opening a drawer, he pulled out two identically shaped packages.

The girls tore open the wrapping. "Cameras!" Trina exclaimed in delight.

"Wow!" Sarah cried out. "These are fancy ones!"

They each hugged both parents and thanked them. "These cameras are as much for us as they are for you," Trina's mother said. "This way, we can share all your experiences when you come back."

"Now, would you like to hear a little more about the ancient ruins?" Dr. Fine asked.

Her mother smiled. "I think they've had enough lessons, Martin."

Dr. Fine frowned. "But we haven't even touched on art and architecture yet."

"Don't worry, Dad," Sarah reassured him. "Honestly, we'll look at *everything*. Every temple and statue . . ."

"And we'll appreciate them all too," Trina added. "I promise!"

"But how will you know what you're looking at?" Dr. Fine asked.

Sarah grinned. "Hey, we've got cameras now. We'll take lots of pictures."

Trina nodded. "And when we get back, you can tell us what we took pictures of."

Dr. Fine scratched his head. "But if you don't first learn what's important to see, how will you know which sights to photograph?"

"Easy," Sarah said. "We'll photograph *everything.*"

Dr. Fine sighed. Then he started pulling on his jacket.

"Where are you going, dear?" his wife asked.

"To buy them more film," he muttered. "If they're going to take pictures of everything they see in Italy, I figure they'll need a thousand rolls. Each!"

Chapter 3

"Girls! Girls!"

In the noise and commotion of the airport, Carolyn's voice could barely be heard. The tall, fair-haired counselor clapped her hands and spoke louder. "Girls, listen to me!"

Standing in line to check luggage, Erin heard the squeals and giggles behind her subside. Along with the other cabin six girls, she gave her attention to Carolyn.

"I'm passing out identification tags for your suitcases, if you don't already have one on them."

Erin brushed an imaginary speck of dust off her brand-new suitcase, and admired it. The shiny red leather smelled wonderful and looked even better, really elegant.

Carolyn handed Erin a tag. Erin examined it and frowned. It was the kind you peeled off and stuck on your bag. It would leave sticky white stuff on the nice leather. She crumpled it and stuck it in her pocket. She didn't need it. She'd have no trouble identifying *her* bag.

Behind her, Katie let out a whoop. "Guys, get a load of this." She read from a book she'd bought in the airport magazine store. "In ancient times, the young girls who tended the fires in the Tempio di Vesta were forbidden to have relationships with men. The traditional punishment for breaking the vow was to be buried alive."

"Ooh, gross!" Megan yelped.

"Another lesson," Sarah murmured. "Katie, you're as bad as my father."

Trina grinned. "But now that we're actually on our way, that stuff is starting to sound really interesting."

Carolyn was busily handing each girl her ticket as the line inched forward. "Have you all got your passports?"

Erin looked at her new purse, especially designed for travel, and pulled the passport out of its own special pocket. "What do we need these for, anyway?"

"You have to carry a passport when you travel out of the country," Carolyn explained. "It proves that you're a citizen of the United

States. You show it to an official person each time you leave a country and enter a country."

Megan read aloud from her passport. " 'The Secretary of State of the United States of America hereby requests all whom it may concern to permit the citizen/national of the United States named herein to pass without delay or hindrance and in case of need to give all lawful aid and protection.' Gee, that's nice. It makes me feel sort of important."

"It should," Carolyn told her. "Remember, when you're visiting another country, you become a representative of the United States. I hope you'll all remember that when you meet people in Italy. If you behave badly, people might think all Americans are awful people."

"What happens if you lose your passport?" Megan asked.

"They probably don't let you back into the United States," Erin told her. Immediately, she knew it was mean of her to have said that. Megan was famous for losing things.

Megan went pale. "Carolyn, is that true? If you lose your passport, you can't go home?"

"No, no. If you lose your passport, you just go to the American consulate."

"I was just teasing you," Erin said kindly. Ac-

35

tually, she too was relieved by Carolyn's words. She'd been known to lose a thing or two herself.

The woman in front of her moved away, and Erin found herself at the counter. "Good evening," the smiling uniformed woman said. "May I see your ticket and passport?"

Erin handed them over, and placed her suitcase on the side of the desk, where it was weighed. The woman tied a red tag to the handle. "That's to make sure your suitcase goes where you go," she explained to Erin. She wrote something on the ticket, and handed it with the passport back to Erin. "Gate fifty-two."

Moving away, Erin noticed a little gift shop, and started toward it.

"Erin!"

She turned, and saw Carolyn beckoning toward her. "Don't get away from the group," the counselor said. "Let's all stay together."

Erin obeyed. But inside, she was wondering if Carolyn planned to watch them all like a hawk throughout this trip. Back at Camp Sunnyside, the girls were always coming up with ways to sneak around and escape Carolyn's attention. Something told her that this wasn't going to be quite so easy in Italy.

When they all finished checking their luggage, Carolyn led them to a hallway where guards stood by a conveyor belt. They had to place their purses and anything else they were carrying on the belt to have them x-rayed.

"Why are you doing that?" Megan asked a guard.

"It's a safety precaution," he told her. "Just to make sure nobody's bringing anything dangerous on the plane."

Megan giggled. "We're bringing Katie. That's pretty dangerous."

Katie gave her a light shove, and Megan shoved back. Then they both started giggling.

"Honestly, you guys," Erin groaned. *"Try* to act mature, okay? Remember what Carolyn said. Do you want the Italians to think we're all goofy?"

They followed Carolyn past the numbered gates until they reached the area marked fifty-two. Megan ran to the window. "Is that our plane?" she asked excitedly. The others joined her. Erin sat down and looked around.

She saw a couple of handsome men, talking rapidly in a language she guessed was Italian. She wondered if all Italians were that good-looking.

She sank back in her seat and smiled happily. This was great! She still couldn't believe her parents had been willing to send her to Italy.

And even though the cabin six girls could be pretty silly, she was glad to be with them instead of a bunch of strangers.

Here she was, on her way to a foreign country. Her friends had been thrilled and envious when she told them. And she much preferred to be envied than felt sorry for! She knew the word would get back to Carla. She'd be furious that Erin was getting to Italy before her! Maybe she'd meet some really cute Italian boy, and she could bring back pictures of him to show around. Carla would be *green*.

Trina sat down beside her with a book in hand, and Katie took the seat next to her. Erin watched curiously as Trina read something, then closed her eyes and moved her lips.

"What are you doing?"

"Practicing Italian," Trina said. *"Buona sera, Signorina* Chapman."

Erin was impressed. "You know how to speak Italian?"

Trina grinned. "No. But I thought it would be polite to be able to say things like 'good day' and 'please' and 'thank you' to the Italian people we meet."

"I can speak Italian," Katie announced.

"You can?" Trina asked in surprise.

"Sure." Katie grinned. "Macaroni, lasagna, ravioli . . ."

Actually, Erin thought Trina's idea was a good one. It certainly would make it easier to meet people. "How do you say 'what is your name?' "

Trina flipped through her phrase book. "Here it is. *'Come si chiama?'* "

Erin practiced it. *"Come si chiama, come si chiama . . ."* It was a start.

Then a voice boomed over the room. "Flight four twenty-eight to Rome, now boarding at gate fifty-two."

"That's us!" Katie yelled.

Carolyn rose. She spoke calmly, but she looked excited too. "Come on, girls."

Megan was hopping up and down. Erin thought she was acting ridiculous. But she had to admit her own insides were hopping up and down too.

They went down a passageway and into the plane, where a flight attendant looked at their boarding passes and directed them to seats. The seats were three across. To make up for her mean remark about the passport, Erin let Megan have the window seat. She went into the middle, and Carolyn took the aisle seat. Sarah, Trina, and Katie sat in the row behind them.

39

She heard Katie tell Trina, "You can have the window seat if you like."

Trina replied, "*Grazie,* Katie. That means thank you in Italian."

Megan twisted around in her seat. "Wow, Trina, you're getting good. By the time we get there, you're going to know the whole language!"

"I've already memorized the most important sentence we need to be able to say," Sarah announced.

"What's that?" Trina asked.

Carefully, Sarah said, "*Dov'é il gabinetto.*"

"What does it mean?" Katie asked.

Sarah grinned. "Where's the bathroom."

They all started giggling again. Erin leaned back in her seat and sighed wearily. Couldn't they at least fake a little sophistication?

Moments later, she forgot all about acting sophisticated herself. Through a loudspeaker, the pilot told the passengers to fasten their seat belts. The plane began to move, picking up speed. Erin gripped her armrests and stared across Megan out the window. They went faster and faster. They were leaving the ground! They were rising higher and higher!

"We're off!" Carolyn exclaimed. "Camp Sunnyside is in the sky!"

"Hey, you know what we should call ourselves in Italy?" Megan cried out excitedly. "Camp Spaghetti!"

Katie let out a cheer. Even Erin was beaming.

Once they were up in the air, the seat belt sign went off. A flight attendant came down the aisle, offering drinks and passing out headsets for the movie that would be shown later. Soon after, dinner was served.

"Boy, this is great," Megan enthused. "Free food, free sodas, and a free movie. I *like* flying!"

So did Erin. It was nice just sitting there, having all these attendants waiting on her. One of the attendants was an Italian man, and like the two she had seen in the waiting area, he was great looking. Her suspicions seemed to be proving true. Italian men were gorgeous. And if the men were gorgeous, the boys must be, too.

She closed her eyes, and started visualizing a younger version of the men she'd seen. Maybe she'd be having a springtime romance after all. . . .

"Erin. Erin!"

She opened her eyes. Carolyn was smiling.

"We're about to land."

Erin stared at her in bewilderment. It was supposed to be a seven-hour ride!

41

"You fell asleep," Carolyn told her. "Lucky you! None of the rest of us did. You'll be the only one who doesn't suffer from jet lag."

"What's jet lag?" Megan asked.

Carolyn began adjusting her watch. "It's now seven-thirty in the morning, Italian time. But your body thinks it's one-thirty in the morning."

Megan yawned. "You know, now I'm getting sleepy."

"Well, you can't sleep now," Carolyn said. She gazed out the window. Megan did too, and gasped.

"We're here!"

There were a few little bumps as the plane landed, and then it began to slow down. Behind her, Erin could hear Katie and Trina and Sarah, clapping and cheering. It was all Erin could do to keep from joining in. She couldn't remember ever feeling so thrilled in her life.

The plane moved slower and slower. Then it came to a full stop.

Megan was still staring out the window. "It looks just like the United States," she said in a disappointed voice.

"That's what you think now," Carolyn said. "All airports look alike. You just wait!"

Suddenly, all the passengers were standing

up, gathering their things and opening the over-head compartments. "Stay together, girls," Carolyn called. They filed out of the plane, followed the crowd, and found themselves in a long line.

"Get out your passports," Carolyn told them. One by one, they handed their passports over to a serious-looking man, who examined them carefully, and then stamped them.

"Now where do we go?" Megan asked.

Carolyn looked around. Then she spotted a sign. "This way." They followed the signs to the carousel where their baggage would arrive.

"Here they come now," Katie said. She hurried forward and grabbed her suitcase. The others hurried around looking for theirs.

Erin watched all the different suitcases moving around the carousel. Then she spotted hers. It was easy—the shiny red leather stood out.

Once they all had their bags, they headed toward the exit. "Erin's parents arranged to have a car meet us, to take us to our hotel."

Trina was the first to see the man holding a sign that read Chapman. As soon as Carolyn identified them, he bowed his head. *"Benvenuto, signorinas!"*

Carolyn interpreted for the girls. "That means welcome, young ladies."

"Grazie!" Trina said shyly, and she was re-

warded with a broad smile. Within seconds, he was ushering them into a minivan, and they were moving.

Even their driver was cute, Erin marveled. Italy was going to be fantastic! Of course, it might not be so easy striking up a relationship with an Italian boy—not with all her giggling cabin mates around and Carolyn watching them. But somehow, she'd find a way.

"Look!" Sarah cried out.

For one fleeting moment, all thoughts of boys and romance evaporated from Erin's mind. There, off in the distance, way up on a hill, stood a whole bunch of strange-looking buildings, or actually, just parts of buildings. They were very, very old, but there was something so beautiful about them, all bathed in a golden light from the sun.

A hush fell over the group as they looked at the ancient site. "That's where the history of Rome begins," Carolyn said in a whisper. "Much of what you're seeing is a thousand years old. It's called the Palatine Hill."

Erin gazed at it in awe. Whatever it was called—there was certainly nothing like it in Pennsylvania!

Chapter 4

It wasn't like any hotel Erin had ever seen before. Whenever she went away on a trip with her parents, they stayed at big, fancy, modern places with glass elevators, fountains in the lobby, and a swimming pool—sometimes two. Erin always liked calling room service in the morning and having her breakfast delivered to her in bed.

The Pensione Polloni didn't look as if it would provide that kind of luxury. It rose only four stories above a crooked narrow street. From the outside, it looked gray and kind of dirty. And while it didn't look as old as those buildings on the Palatine Hill, it wasn't exactly new.

Carolyn, at least, seemed very pleased as they emerged from the van. "Oh, it's charming!" she exclaimed. The others all just gazed at it with

45

glassy expressions. Erin suspected they were all feeling a little out of it.

She couldn't blame them. Remembering what Carolyn had said earlier, she checked her watch. It might be nine in the morning here, but if they were back home, they'd all be sound asleep.

The driver helped them bring their luggage inside. Then with a cheery *"arrivederci"* he was gone.

Erin looked around in dismay at the lobby— if you could even call it that. There were no elevators, no fountain, no lounge. It was just a tiny room with a worn-looking bench and some pictures on the walls.

"Benvenuto! Welcome to the Pensione Polloni!"

Erin turned, and automatically her spirits lifted a bit. Behind a counter stood the most incredibly handsome boy. Okay, maybe he wasn't a boy. A young man. He had curly black hair, dark flashing eyes, and a warm smile.

"Good morning," Carolyn said. "I'm Carolyn Lewis. I believe you have reservations for us."

The man checked a book. "Ah yes, from America! I will gather the keys and show you to your rooms."

His accent was charming, and if possible, it made him look even better. He could be a movie star, Erin thought. What was he doing working in a hotel?

The other girls were gaping at him. Erin wished she could think of something to say to make her stand out. In a flash of inspiration, she recalled what Trina had taught her.

She stepped forward. *"Come si chiama?"*

His eyes lit up. And from his mouth burst forth a torrent of Italian.

Erin stepped back in utter confusion. "Huh?"

"I'm sorry, she doesn't speak Italian," Carolyn said. "None of us do, really. But the girls have been learning a few words and phrases."

"A very fine idea," the man said with approval. "Allow me to introduce myself. I am Enrico Polloni."

"Buon giorno, Signor Polloni," Trina said shyly.

"Per favore, please, you will call me Enrico."

"Then this is your hotel?" Katie asked.

"It belongs to my parents," Enrico told them. "I assist them when I am on holiday from the university." He came out from behind the counter, holding three old-fashioned keys. "You will follow me, yes?"

He led them up a flight of stairs. "There are three rooms on this floor," he told them. "One contains three beds, one has two beds, and the last is for one person."

Erin knew the single room would have to be Carolyn's. Quickly, she considered who she would want to room with. Trina could be a real goody-goody sometimes. Katie was awfully bossy. And Sarah liked to read at night with the light on.

"Megan and I will take the double room," she announced.

Enrico opened a door. "This is the room for two." Erin and Megan entered.

Megan seemed to come out of her daze for a moment. "Ooh, this is neat!" She went over to the wall where curtains covered double doors. She opened them. "Look, Erin! It's a balcony!"

Erin joined her. The balcony looked over a courtyard. It was actually sort of pretty. Then she examined the room. It certainly wasn't as big as the ones she usually stayed in with her parents. The furniture looked old, and there wasn't any little refrigerator stocked with goodies. There wasn't even a television or telephone! That was okay, she decided. She wouldn't be able to understand Italian television anyway. And she didn't know anyone in Rome to call on the phone.

At least it was neat and clean. In the corner,

she saw a door leading to a bathroom. There were flowers on the dresser and pictures on the wall. And the two twin beds were covered with pretty blue spreads.

Megan was looking at the beds longingly. Then she yawned. "I'm going to lie down for a minute." She crawled onto one of the beds.

Carolyn appeared at the door. She looked sleepy too. "I think Megan has the right idea. Why don't we all have a little nap?" A yawn escaped her lips. "I'll come wake everyone up in about two hours."

"Okay," Erin said. Megan's eyes were already closed, and she was breathing evenly. Despite her own nap on the plane, Erin was feeling a little tired herself.

But she felt something else too. Grimy. It seemed like a long time since she'd had a bath or a shower, and she decided to do that first before her nap.

She went into the bathroom. The tub was like the kind in her grandmother's house, with funny-looking feet, and there wasn't a real shower—just an attachment spray thing you held by hand. It took some fiddling and experimenting to figure out how to turn the water on.

She filled the tub and got in. As she soaked, she thought about Enrico. She couldn't remember ever having such a handsome man in her life. Of course, if he was a student at a university, he was probably at least eighteen. She sighed. Oh well, she thought, at least she could fantasize.

When she got out of the tub and wrapped herself in a towel, she felt much better. In fact, the idea of taking a nap wasn't even appealing anymore.

But what was she going to do for two hours while the others were sleeping? She decided she might as well unpack. She lifted her suitcase from the floor. It felt heavier than it had earlier, she thought.

Laying it on her bed, she fumbled with the locks. Funny, she didn't remember having trouble turning the clasp before.

Finally, she got it open. And then she gasped.

This wasn't her suitcase.

Chapter 5

Frozen, her skin prickling, Erin stared at the contents of the suitcase. This just couldn't be true. Was she dreaming? Hallucinating? She closed her eyes and opened them again.

She saw none of her clothes, no shoes, no blow dryer. Inside the suitcase lay something gold and silver. She pulled it out. It looked like an evening gown, or maybe a bathrobe. Underneath, there was a wig of long brown hair. And under that was an array of bottles and jars and compacts, sponges and brushes and tubes.

She picked up a bottle. The label was Italian, and she couldn't read it, but what was inside looked like makeup. She took a jar. Again, she couldn't make out the words on it, but opening it she got a whiff of cold cream.

She felt numb all over. Somehow, she managed to close the case. She searched the outside for something that would identify the owner. But there was nothing. It was just like hers.

Maybe it had all been an illusion. She opened the suitcase again. The same collection of stuff greeted her. She checked a few more items. There were tons of lipsticks, some pink and red creams, and several sets of false eyelashes.

She became aware that her heart was pounding rapidly. She clutched her towel closer. What was she going to do?

The answer was obvious. She was going to have to wake Carolyn and tell her. Her heart sank at the idea. Carolyn would want to know why she hadn't checked the label on the suitcase before taking it from the carousel at the airport. Erin would have to confess that she hadn't put a label on her own suitcase. Carolyn would be furious, and Erin would have to listen to Carolyn's lecture and I told you so. It would be so humiliating!

But what else could she do? All her clothes were gone! And she had no idea how to get her own suitcase back. She steeled herself to endure Carolyn's anger—and then she had another notion.

Situations like this must happen all the time when people arrived at hotels. The guy downstairs—Enrico. He'd know what to do. And telling him, a complete stranger, would be a lot easier than facing Carolyn.

She headed for the door, and almost walked out before realizing she was still wrapped in a towel. She hurried back to the bathroom and eyed her clothes on the floor with distaste. She hated the thought of putting the wrinkled pants and shirt back on, but she had no choice.

She dressed quickly and glanced in the mirror. I look pale, she thought. Thank goodness she had a makeup kit in her purse. Even in her panic, she couldn't bear the thought of that handsome man seeing her looking so bad.

As she applied some lipstick, she saw the open suitcase through the mirror. Whoever it belonged to certainly used a lot of makeup.

She left the room and hurried downstairs. Enrico greeted her with a smile, which drooped a bit when he caught her expression. "Is something wrong, *signorina?*"

Erin tried to smile, but in her panic it wasn't easy. "I—I picked up the wrong suitcase at the airport!"

Enrico said something in Italian that Erin couldn't understand, but she recognized the dismay in his tone.

He must think I'm an idiot, Erin thought mournfully. "It looked just like mine," she ex-

53

plained. "And I'll bet that whoever it belongs to has my suitcase."

Enrico nodded sympathetically. "Yes, of course. Then we shall examine the suitcase for identification, and contact this person."

"I looked already," Erin told him. "There's no name on the suitcase."

"Hm," Enrico murmured. "Then I am certain the person who has your suitcase will contact you."

Erin shook her head miserably. "I didn't put any identification on mine either."

She could have sworn she caught a brief look of disapproval on his face. But at least he didn't wag his finger in her face and start a lecture. "This is a problem," he said.

"It's a big problem!" Erin exclaimed. "I don't have anything but the clothes I'm wearing. I don't even have a toothbrush!" She became suddenly aware of a sour taste in her mouth and an enormous desire to brush her teeth.

"Have you informed *Signorina* Lewis?"

"Carolyn? No, she's having a nap. I . . . um, I didn't want to disturb her. She's older, you know. She needs her rest."

A smile flickered on his face. "I see." Just then, an older man entered the hotel.

"Ah, *papà*," Enrico greeted him. He began

54

speaking rapidly in Italian. Erin figured he must be telling his father about her problem, because the older man turned to her sadly with a reproving look. Then, in Italian, he spoke to Enrico.

"My father doesn't speak English," Enrico explained to Erin. "He has a suggestion. He will call the airport. It is hoped that the person who has your suitcase will do the same, and the airport can contact us here."

Erin breathed a deep sigh of relief. She described the suitcase and its contents to Enrico, who then translated the description into Italian for his father.

Erin's panic practically disappeared. She'd still have to tell Carolyn, probably, but now that a plan was in action to get her case back she wasn't so upset. Why, she'd probably have her own suitcase back today. She sort of hoped she'd meet the woman who took hers. She was curious to see what kind of person would need so much makeup.

But it was possible she wouldn't get her suitcase back until tomorrow. And there were still some things she couldn't wait any longer to have. "Is there someplace I can buy some stuff?" she asked Enrico. "Like a toothbrush, and . . ." She blushed. She couldn't very well tell him she needed underwear. "Uh, other stuff."

"Of course," Enrico said. "There is a large department store nearby. But this is your first time in Rome, yes? It would not be good for you to attempt to find the store. You could get lost."

Erin frowned. But Enrico's next words turned the frown around. "I shall escort you."

"Oh, thank you!" So every cloud really did have a silver lining. She may have lost her suitcase, but she was going to walk around Rome with a handsome guy—and without a bunch of screeching cabin mates.

"I'll go get my pocketbook and be right back," Erin told him. As she hurried toward the stairs, he called out to her. "And be certain to let Miss Lewis know where you are going."

In the room, Megan was still sleeping. Tiptoeing, Erin found her pocketbook and left. In the hallway, she hesitated, and glanced at Carolyn's door. Then she shrugged. Why disturb her? She'd be back before Carolyn woke up. She ran down the stairs to join Enrico.

Enrico had super manners. He held the door open for Erin. Then he took her arm as they walked up the street.

"*Signorina,* it occurs to me that I do not know your name," he said.

56

Personally, Erin was perfectly happy to be called *signorina*. It sounded so elegant. But of course, that's what they called all girls here. "I'm Erin. Erin Chapman."

"Erin," he repeated. He trilled the *r* in her name, and it sounded so pretty! Everything he did and said intrigued her. He was nothing like the guys back home.

She was so busy thinking about him that she barely noticed the unfamiliar buildings and sights—until they got to the end of the street and entered a huge square.

"Wow! What's that?" Erin stared straight ahead at stairs that seemed to stretch a whole block, and went up so high she could barely make out the people sitting on them.

"We are in the Piazza di Spagna," Enrico told her. "Those are the Spanish Steps."

"Why are all those people sitting on them?"

"Because it is very pleasant to watch the world go by. I myself sometimes sit there on a warm evening after dinner, and eat a *gelato*."

A *gelato*. That sounded very exotic. Erin wondered what it was. She didn't want to ask, though. Already, she was worrying that she sounded like just another gawking tourist. "I love *gelato*," she said.

Enrico smiled. "Then you must allow me to treat you to one while you are visiting."

Erin's eyes widened. Back home, when a boy treated a girl to something, it meant . . . well, it was like a date. Was it possible that Enrico was suggesting they have a date? No, it couldn't be. He was so much older than she was. But even so . . . she just hoped that whatever *gelato* was, it wouldn't be too disgusting.

Just before they arrived at the department store, Enrico asked, "Do you have money for your purchases?"

Erin had checked her wallet before she left. "I've got traveler's checks, and fifty dollars in cash."

"But you must have Italian money, lire, to purchase items here," he told her. "Look, there is a bank. They will exchange the money for you."

They went into the bank, and Enrico directed her to the appropriate person. Erin signed a traveler's check, and gave it to the cashier. A few seconds later, he gave her a stack of bills. She joined Enrico.

Just as she was about to stuff the money in her wallet, something hit her eye—the number in the corner of the bills. For what seemed like the zillionth time that day, she gasped. "Enrico, that man made a big mistake! That was only a fifty-dollar traveler's check that I gave him. And he's given me back thousands!"

Enrico chuckled. "It is the rate of exchange, Erin. One American dollar is worth more than one thousand lire."

Erin blushed. She should have known that. "You must think I'm awfully dumb."

"Not at all," Enrico said. "I find you very . . . how would you say it in English? Yes, enchanting."

Enchanting. Erin wanted to swoon. No one had ever called her enchanting in her life.

The department store, at least, didn't look very different from any department store back home. With Enrico's help, Erin was able to find everything she needed—toothbrush and toothpaste, shampoo, underwear—and she had enough money left over for a simple tee shirt.

Leaving the store, Erin felt a lot better. Gazing around, she began to appreciate the beauty of her surroundings—a lovely fountain with statues around it, a church that looked more like a fairy-tale castle. She noticed a couple, walking slowly, arm in arm.

She sighed. "Rome looks like a very romantic city. Maybe that's where the word romantic came from."

"Ah yes," Enrico said. "We are certainly a romantic people. I hope you will be able to explore our city."

Erin nodded. "I want to see *everything.*"

"And so you should. But you must stay with your group, and not walk alone."

"Why not?" Erin asked.

"Well, for a beautiful young lady like yourself, Rome can be a dangerous place."

Erin had stopped listening after the words "beautiful young lady." A shiver went through her. He didn't think she was a cute kid, or even a pretty girl. A beautiful young lady—wow!

Enrico continued. "You must always remember that you are in a different culture, one that is not familiar to you. I have never been to the United States, but perhaps you will find that men here may behave in a different way."

At first, Erin wasn't sure what he meant. Then it hit her. He was saying that here, in Rome, it wasn't so odd for an older guy to be attracted to a younger girl. Maybe back in Pennsylvania, a university student wouldn't pay much attention to a twelve-year-old girl. But here in Rome—it was actually a possibility! And what was that saying she'd heard—when in Rome, do as the Romans do. That sounded like a good idea to her.

Enrico opened the door for her at the Pensione Polloni. Erin floated inside. Then she winced.

Carolyn was at the desk, her face pale and anxious. She was waving her arms as she talked to Enrico's father. At least, she was trying to talk to him. From the bewildered look on Mr. Polloni's face, it was obvious that he didn't understand a word Carolyn was saying.

When Carolyn turned and saw Erin, relief flooded her face. "Thank goodness!" And then the relief turned to anger. "Erin, you had me frantic! Where have you been? I told you to stay with the group!"

Erin squirmed. Did she have to talk to her like she was a child?

Enrico spoke soothingly. "She's quite all right, Miss Lewis. She needed some items so I took her to a store." He turned to Erin. "Didn't you leave her a note?"

Erin bit her lip. "I guess I was so upset, I forgot."

Carolyn ran her fingers through her disheveled hair. "Upset about what?"

Erin took a deep breath. Then she told Carolyn about the suitcase mix-up.

"Are you telling me you didn't put a tag on your suitcase? Erin, I specifically told you to do that! Do you realize what a foolish thing you've done?"

Erin wanted to sink into a hole in the ground. What would Enrico think, hearing Carolyn speak to her like that?

But Enrico remained calm. "We have taken steps to recover it, Miss Lewis, and—"

Carolyn didn't let him finish. She shifted her angry eyes from Erin to Enrico. "You had no business taking her anywhere without informing me. She's my responsibility! Do you have any idea how upset I was, walking into the room and finding her missing?"

"I apologize sincerely," Enrico replied. "I was under the impression that you knew where she was going."

Carolyn's face was still tense, but she calmed down a little. "Yes, yes, all right. Erin, what are we going to do about your suitcase?"

"My father has informed the airport," Enrico said. He turned to Mr. Polloni and spoke in Italian. His father replied. Even though Erin couldn't understand him, she could tell from his expression and gestures that the news wasn't good.

"My father says there has been no report yet at the airport from the person who has Erin's suitcase. May I make a suggestion?"

62

"Yes?" Carolyn asked coldly.

"Let us examine the suitcase Erin has. Perhaps we will find some indication inside of the ownership."

Carolyn agreed, and they went upstairs to Erin's room.

Megan, Katie, Sarah, and Trina were all gathered in the one room. "Thank goodness!" Katie cried out.

Megan actually looked like she might have been crying. "We were so worried!"

Erin attempted to look blasé. "I just had to pick up a few things." While Carolyn and Enrico began to search through the suitcase, she told the others what had happened.

"This is very fancy, whatever it is," Carolyn said, looking at the golden gown.

"What's that?" Trina asked. She pointed to a scrap of paper that had just fallen out. Enrico picked it up.

"It appears to be a piece of a credit card receipt," he said. "It's very faint, and I cannot make out the numbers. But there's the part of a name—"

Carolyn peered at it. "That looks like . . . Bellini?"

Trina joined them. "And the first name begins with a *c*."

Enrico nodded. "I tell you what we shall do now. We will go downstairs and get a telephone directory. And attempt to locate this *Signorina* Bellini."

"Bellini," Erin said. "That sounds like an unusual name."

Enrico smiled, but he shook his head. "Unfortunately, not in Italy."

Chapter 6

They all gathered in a small office behind the hotel reception desk, where there was a telephone. The Rome telephone directory was the fattest one Erin had ever seen. And Enrico was right. There were *lots* of Bellinis.

Enrico began to dial. With each call, he asked in Italian to speak with *Signora* or *Signorina* Bellini. Sometimes, there was only a *Signor* Bellini. With some of the attempts, there was no answer to the call. Enrico did reach some women named Bellini, but none of them had lost a suitcase.

After twenty minutes of calling, Enrico was only halfway down the list of Bellinis with first names beginning with *C.* Erin was beginning to feel very sorry for him. Carolyn, too, seemed to have forgiven him for taking Erin out.

"This is very kind of you, *Signor* Polloni," she said.

"Not at all, Miss Lewis," he said gallantly. "Please, call me Enrico."

"And I'm Carolyn. I'm afraid we're taking up a lot of your time."

"It is not a problem," Enrico said, and began dialing another number.

"You know," Trina said, "if this Bellini woman is married, the listing could be under another first name."

Enrico, holding the phone to his ear, nodded glumly. "There is no response at this number," he declared, hanging up. He made a pencil mark next to the name in his book. "We shall have to try that one again later."

Sarah glanced at the window. "The sun is shining. It looks like a beautiful day."

Erin could feel reproachful eyes settling on her. Their first day in Rome, and they'd be spending it watching Enrico telephoning. And it was all her fault.

Carolyn nodded. "Yes, I think we should stop calling for a while, and go out."

There was no mistaking the relief on Enrico's face. "I could make more calls for you later. Or perhaps it will not be necessary. This woman will certainly discover her mistake and call the airport."

"That's right," Carolyn said. "Well, girls, what shall we see first?" She fished a fat book out of her purse. "I have a guide right here."

"Oh, no," Enrico protested. "You must not rely on a guidebook. You should have a personal guide, a real Italian, to show you Rome."

"And how are we supposed to find a real Italian guide to Rome?" Carolyn asked.

Enrico rose from his chair, smiled, and bowed. "At your service, *signorinas.*"

Erin caught her breath. He wanted to spend the day with them! She looked at Carolyn hopefully.

"Oh, but we can't impose on you," Carolyn objected.

"It would be a pleasure," Enrico insisted. "This is my city, and I wish to share its glory with you." His eyes encircled the group, but Erin could have sworn they lingered a second or two longer on *her.*

Carolyn seemed uncertain. Then she relented. "Well, it would be nice to have a native with us."

Enrico led them outside. They paused at a newsstand to buy bus tickets, and then headed toward the bus stop. To do so, they had to cross a large street.

Megan gaped at the traffic before them. "Those cars are going *fast!*"

"Yes, you must be very careful when crossing streets in Rome," Enrico told her. "Actually, I suggest holding hands to cross the street."

Katie grabbed Trina's hand and plunged into the chaos. Carolyn took Sarah with one hand, and Megan with the other. With a thrill, Erin realized that left only her and Enrico. And when Enrico took her hand, she shivered. Had he actually maneuvered himself to be by her side?

A bus approached just as they arrived at the stop, and they got on. Desperately, Erin tried to work it out so she'd be sitting with Enrico, but he slid into a seat next to Carolyn. Oh well, she thought, he has to be polite.

It wasn't a long ride. "We shall begin our tour where Rome itself began," Enrico told them when they got off the bus. "The Campidoglio, the capitol itself."

"I thought Rome was the capital," Katie said.

"This is the ancient capitol," Trina told her. "I read about it. It was restored in 1537 by Michelangelo."

Erin groaned inwardly. She hoped Trina

didn't plan to lecture them on the history of Rome all day.

She didn't—but Enrico did. He seemed to know everything about the buildings and churches and statues that they saw on the hill. He told them how this was one of the seven hills on which Rome was built.

"Oh yeah, we saw one of those hills on the way from the airport," Sarah noted.

"That was the Palatine Hill," Enrico said. "The home of Romulus."

"Romulus," Erin repeated. "Is he a friend of yours?"

Enrico tossed back his head and laughed. But it was a nice laugh, not a mocking one. "Romulus was the founder of Roma, this city you call Rome. Do you not know the legend of Romulus and Remus?"

"I do," Sarah cried out. "I read it in my Roman mythology book. They were twins, right?"

"Yes," Enrico said. "They were the sons of the god Mars, but they were raised on the banks of the Tiber River by a wolf. They built a city, which became Roma, named for Romulus."

"Why wasn't it named for Remus?" Megan asked.

"Because, during a quarrel, Romulus killed Remus," Enrico told them.

Trina was horrified. "He killed his own twin brother? That's terrible!"

"Those were the olden days," Erin stated. "People did things like that."

"Erin is right," Enrico said. Erin glowed. "The ancient Romans were a brutal people."

They walked on, and soon arrived at an area that looked like a real mess to Erin. Crumbling buildings with no roofs, columns that supported nothing, and a lot of broken-up statues were all over the place.

"This is the Roman Forum," Enrico announced. "Once, what you see here was the very heart of Rome."

"It doesn't look like much now," Katie commented.

"Try to imagine what it looked like fifteen hundred years ago," Enrico told the girls. "It was filled with temples and palaces and shops. It was the center of the city. People gathered here from all over."

Erin gazed around, but her imagination was limited. Still, for Enrico's sake, she pretended to appreciate it. "Yes, I can picture it now! It must have been very grand."

Enrico led them around, pointing out this and that. As much as Erin loved the sound of his voice, it was all getting a little boring.

As they walked along, Enrico pointed to the ruins of a small, circular building. "This is the Temple of Vesta," he began, but Katie interrupted him.

"Hey, that's the one I was reading about! Remember, you guys? They tended the fire, and if one of the Vestals was found with a guy, she was buried alive!"

"And the man who was involved with the Vestal was stoned to death," Enrico added.

Trina shuddered. "Why would any girl take a chance like that?"

"Who can say," Enrico pondered. "Perhaps, if two people were very much in love, they were willing to take the risk and break the law. When there is true love, rules become unimportant; they are meaningless."

Erin looked straight into his eyes as he spoke. He smiled at her. And she felt that shiver again. Was there a special meaning in what he'd just said?

Then she noticed Carolyn looking at him oddly. Of course, Carolyn would disapprove of any hint of something going on between Enrico and Erin.

Then she realized what she was thinking, and she felt silly. Stop it, Erin, she warned herself sternly. You're letting your imagination run

71

away with you. Nothing's going on between you and Enrico. Yet.

From the Roman Forum, they went across a street to a humongous round building that looked like a stadium. "This is the Colosseum, the most remarkable monument of ancient Rome," Enrico told them. "It was built in the first century."

"You mean it's almost two thousand years old?" Sarah asked, her eyes wide.

Well, that explained all the broken tiers and ledges, Erin thought. They were standing on an upper level of the arena. "More than fifty thousand spectators gathered here," Enrico said.

"For what?" Megan asked. "Games?"

"Sometimes," Enrico said. "But also for battles between gladiators and wild beasts."

Erin leaned over the railing, and tried to imagine the battles below. It was dizzying, looking down like that. Then she felt Enrico's hands on her shoulders. "Do not lean too far, my dear," he said. "I would not wish to lose you." With that, Erin thought she really might faint.

"Is anyone else getting hungry?" Trina asked.

"Yes, I think it's about time for lunch," Carolyn said. "Enrico, do you know a place to eat near here?"

"I know just the place," Enrico said. "Since

it's such a warm and lovely day, I think we should dine alfresco."

What was alfresco, Erin wondered. Some kind of Italian food? "I just love alfresco," she said.

Carolyn's lips twitched. "I didn't know you loved eating out of doors, Erin."

Erin flushed. So that was what alfresco meant. Thank goodness Carolyn had warned her. What if she'd ordered "alfresco" in the restaurant and made a total fool of herself in front of Enrico?

In a square near the Colosseum, they settled at a large table. A waiter appeared and handed out menus. "They have pizza here!" Katie exclaimed.

Trina studied the menu. "But I don't understand the names of these different kinds of pizza."

"May I suggest the pizza margherita," Enrico said. "I believe that is the type you will find most familiar."

"What are you having?" Erin asked him.

"I shall have calamari," he told her.

The waiter came to take their orders. The other cabin six girls ordered pizza margherita. Carolyn ordered another kind of pizza, and Enrico ordered calamari.

"I'll have calamari, too," Erin said.

73

Carolyn eyed her curiously. "Are you sure, Erin?"

Erin drew herself up stiffly. "Of course I'm sure!"

"Grazie," the waiter said, and left the table.

"Have you had calamari before?" Carolyn asked Erin.

Erin hesitated. Should she lie? No, one of the other girls might ask what it was, and then she'd really look stupid. "No," she replied honestly. "But I think it's important to try new things when you travel."

"That's an excellent attitude," Enrico said. He gave her a smile of approval. No matter what calamari turned out to be, it was worth ordering to have him look at her that way.

While the others chatted about the sights they'd seen, Erin gazed out into the square. It *was* lovely. The old buildings that surrounded the square had charming little iron balconies. She could just imagine Juliet standing on one, while Romeo declared his love for her from below. In the square, couples passed, walking arm in arm. One couple paused and kissed each other, right there out in the open!

Oh, if only she were alone here with Enrico. If only she could think of another way to get

Enrico to herself! She searched her mind for possible schemes, but nothing came.

She became aware of Carolyn watching her. "Erin, is everything okay?"

"Sure! Why?"

"Well, you've got a strange look on your face."

Enrico leaned over and spoke softly. "Do not worry, Erin. We will locate your suitcase."

Erin smiled. Funny, she'd almost completely forgotten about her lost suitcase! "*Grazie*, Enrico," she murmured.

"Ah, you are learning Italian! That is very fine." His piercing eyes looked directly into her own.

"Erin, are you cold?" Trina asked.

"No, why?"

"You just shivered."

Erin swallowed. Luckily, just then the waiter appeared with their orders. Erin stared uncertainly down at the plate set in front of her. It was a pile of . . . *things*. Some were round, some were squiggly. All Erin could be sure of was that they were fried.

Enrico was eating his mound of round and squiggly fried things with gusto. "Delicious!" he proclaimed. Erin took a tentative bite. The texture was kind of rubbery, but the taste wasn't bad at all. In fact, it was rather nice.

Enrico turned to Carolyn. "What is the name of calamari in English?"

Carolyn glanced uneasily at Erin. She seemed reluctant to answer Enrico, but finally she did. "Squid."

Erin began coughing. Katie reached over and slapped her on the back.

"Are you all right?" Enrico asked anxiously. "Do you not like the . . . how do you say it? Squid?"

Erin recovered. "Oh, no, yes, I like it very much. I just adore"—she gulped—"squid."

Erin's feet were killing her. After lunch, Enrico had taken them to the Vatican, across the Tiber. There, they saw the largest church in the world, St. Peter's, and from there they walked to the Sistine Chapel.

"You must pay special attention to the ceiling," Enrico told them. "In 1508, Michelangelo was commissioned to paint it, lying on his back. It took four years!" By the time they got out of there, Erin's neck was hurting too.

"Enrico, you have been very kind to show us around," Carolyn said as they walked to a bus stop. "But I think we should go back to the hotel now. The girls need a rest before dinner."

"But we must have a *gelato* before you return," Enrico insisted. "I promised Erin I would treat her to a *gelato* while you are all in Rome."

"We can do that another day," Carolyn said. "This is only our first day here, remember?" She looked tired, and so did all the others. Erin couldn't remember ever walking so much, not even on Sunnyside hikes.

"What's a *gelato?*" Megan asked Erin in a whisper.

Erin rolled her eyes. "Oh, Megan, get real."

"Then you must allow me to escort you again tomorrow," Enrico said.

While Carolyn protested, Erin's heart was singing. Surely, Enrico had other things he could do besides lead a bunch of tourists around Rome. Maybe it wasn't just her imagination. Enrico really wanted to be with her!

They took a bus back to the Pensione Polloni. Once again, Erin tried to get herself in a position so she could sit next to Enrico. But again, he was sitting with Carolyn, and she found herself with Sarah.

"That Enrico's really nice, isn't he?" Sarah said.

Erin considered her response. She didn't want the others to know how she was feeling. "He's okay, I guess."

"He thinks *you're* more than okay," Sarah stated.

Erin looked at her sharply. "What do you mean?"

"I heard him tell Carolyn you reminded him of some famous painting. Something about Venus."

Venus. Erin racked her brain. A few years ago in school, they had studied the Roman gods and goddesses. Venus—she was the goddess of beauty!

When they got off the bus, Enrico walked with them back to the hotel. "I want to see if there have been any calls regarding Erin's suitcase," he said.

In the lobby, he spoke to his father in Italian and received a response. Erin could tell from the shaking of his father's head what the response was.

Her heart sank. Enrico would see her tomorrow wearing the same clothes she wore today. "I guess I'll have to get some more clothes," she announced. "I'll call my parents and tell them what happened. They'll send me more money. Enrico, could you take me to some stores tomorrow morning?"

Before Enrico could respond, Carolyn spoke.

"I have a list of shops in my guidebook, Erin. We'll do some shopping in the morning."

Erin smiled thinly. "Okay." As they headed for the stairs, she heard Enrico speak quietly to Carolyn. "May I talk to you for a moment?"

The others were mounting the stairs. Erin ducked behind a large plant that separated the stairs from the lobby. She saw Enrico's lips moving, but she couldn't make out what he was saying to Carolyn.

She could hear Carolyn's response. "No, it's out of the question. I'm sorry."

Enrico's lips were moving again. Erin strained, but it was impossible to hear.

"I'm responsible for these girls," Carolyn said. "I don't think . . . well, let's talk about it tomorrow."

Erin stood very still. She waited until Enrico had left the building, and Carolyn had started up the stairs. Then she came out from behind the plant.

Her heart was thumping wildly. Enrico must have asked Carolyn for permission to see Erin alone. And Carolyn, being the counselor type, had refused.

But Erin didn't care. The important thing was the fact that Enrico was as attracted to her as she was to him. And Erin would figure out somehow, some way to get together with him.

Talk about springtime romances! Never in a million years would Erin have ever thought something like *this* could happen!

Chapter 7

Two days later, Erin was having a delicious dream. She was walking through one of the many piazzas she'd seen, hand in hand with Enrico. They paused before a fountain with cascading water. Enrico looked deeply into her eyes and said something in Italian. It seemed so real. . . .

She opened her eyes. She wasn't in a piazza with Enrico. She was lying in her bed in the *pensione*. From the bathroom, she could hear the sound of water running.

Erin sighed. It was only a dream. And she was getting carried away again. Enrico hadn't really said or done anything to make her think he was madly in love with her. But he'd been with them every day since they arrived in Rome. He'd taken them to see churches, museums, piazzas . . . and when he wasn't acting as a tour guide, he was calling Bellinis. Surely he had other things he could be doing with his time. There had to be a reason why he was hanging out with them.

She sat up in bed and hugged her knees. Megan emerged from the bathroom. "Did they find your suitcase?"

"No," Erin replied. "Why did you think that?"

"You look so happy."

There was a knock on the door. "It's us!" Megan opened it, and Katie, Trina, and Sarah trooped in.

"C'mon, you guys, get dressed," Katie ordered. "We're meeting Carolyn in the breakfast room in five minutes."

Erin reluctantly dragged herself out of bed and went into the bathroom.

"Did Enrico finish calling all the Bellinis in the phone book?" Sarah called out.

Mumbling through a mouth full of toothpaste, Erin replied, "Yeah. And he couldn't find one woman who had lost a suitcase." Returning, she eyed her jeans mournfully. "I can't believe I have to wear the same clothes *again.*"

"What does it matter?" Katie asked. "You don't have to impress *us.*"

"That's right," Sarah said. "It's not as if there were any boys around for you to flirt with."

"Oh no?" Erin pulled on her sweater. "What do you call Enrico? A girl?"

Trina looked shocked. "Erin! Are you saying you have a crush on Enrico? He's not a boy, he's a *man!*"

"Mm." Erin pictured the reaction of her friends back home when they heard about this. She'd have to remember to get a photo of Enrico to show them.

Trina was still shaking her head in disapproval. "Erin, he's much too old for you."

Erin brushed that objection aside. "Maybe back home he would be. But this is Italy. Things are different here."

"That's right," Sarah said thoughtfully. "Juliet was only about thirteen. I think Romeo was older. And that took place in Italy."

"Oh, Erin, this is so romantic!" Megan exclaimed. "You and an older man."

Katie snorted. "This is the dumbest conversation I ever heard. Enrico wouldn't be interested in some *kid.*"

Erin raised her eyebrows. "Yeah? How do you know? You're not exactly experienced in these things."

Katie wasn't insulted. "Let me put it this

way. If Enrico Polloni turns out to be madly in love with Erin Chapman, I'll . . . I'll make your bed every day this summer at Sunnyside."

"Fine," Erin said cheerfully. "I hate making my bed." She paused. "But I may not even go back to Sunnyside this summer. I'm going to ask my parents to look into summer camps here in Italy."

"Girls! Hurry up!" Carolyn's voice from the hallway penetrated the closed door.

"Listen, you guys," Erin said hurriedly. "Not a word about me and Enrico to Carolyn, okay?" There was a general nodding of heads. Katie rolled her eyes and Trina still looked concerned, but Erin wasn't worried. Cabin six girls never revealed secrets to counselors.

They went downstairs to the breakfast room, where they were served hot chocolate and delicious, crunchy rolls. "What are we doing today?" Trina asked Carolyn.

"It's a little gray outside," Carolyn said. "I thought we'd go to the Pantheon. Then, if it clears up, we'll stroll through the Borghese Gardens."

"What's the Pantheon?" Megan asked.

"It's an interesting building from Imperial Rome," Carolyn told them. "I'll have to read you the history of it from the guidebook."

"Maybe Enrico will be able to tell us all about it," Sarah remarked.

Carolyn shook her head. "We can't expect Enrico to go around Rome with us everyday. He's got his own life, you know. I told him we'd be on our own today."

Erin was aware of Katie glancing at her with a smug expression. She rose. "Um, I left something in my room. I'll be right back."

In the lobby, *Signor* Polloni, Enrico's father, was on the telephone. But the door to the office was open, and she could see Enrico in there. She slipped by *Signor* Polloni and stood at the office door. Enrico looked up and flashed that fabulous smile.

"Buon giorno, Erin," he said. "Good morning."

"Good morning. I just heard that you're not going around with us today."

The corners of his mouth turned down slightly. "Yes. Carolyn said it was not necessary for me to join you. Perhaps you are tired of my company."

"Oh no!" Erin exclaimed. "I—we would love to have you with us!"

His eyes lit up. "You would? But Carolyn—"

Erin interrupted. "She just doesn't want to take advantage of you. But I'm sure she'd like

85

you to come with us." She lowered her eyes demurely. "I know *I* would."

He didn't seem to need much convincing. "I will be with you in a moment."

Erin sailed back into the breakfast room. "Enrico's changed his mind. He's coming with us." She shot Katie a triumphant grin.

Carolyn frowned. "Now, Erin, I hope you didn't—" But before she could say more, Enrico entered the room.

"Are you ready for today's tour, *signorinas?*"

Katie gazed at him through narrow eyes. "I thought you had other things to do today."

He smiled. "The charming Erin has convinced me to leave my work. Come! Rome awaits us."

The Pantheon turned out to be a huge circular building with a gigantic dome. Enrico told them about it. "It was first built in 27 B.C., and rebuilt in A.D. 120. Originally, it was designed as a tribute to the ancient Roman gods."

"And the goddesses too, I hope," Carolyn murmured.

"But of course! Juno, Minerva, Venus . . ."

"Venus," Erin said. "She was the goddess of beauty, right?"

"That is correct," Enrico said. "When you go to the city of Florence, you will visit the Uffizi museum. There you will see a famous painting, *The Birth of Venus,* by Botticelli." He paused thoughtfully. "I am reminded of this painting every time I look at Erin. In face and hair, she is most similar."

Katie's mouth dropped open. It was all Erin could do to keep from pinching her and saying, "See?"

When they emerged from the Pantheon, the sun was out. "Let's go to the Borghese Gardens," Carolyn suggested.

Enrico agreed. "But on the way, we must stop at the Trevi Fountain."

"What's so special about the Trevi Fountain?" Katie asked.

"You will see," Enrico replied.

And so they did. The Trevi Fountain was in a tiny piazza, and maybe that's what made it seem so much grander than any of the other fountains they'd seen. But Erin could see there was something special about the stone sea creatures that were surrounded by water.

Carolyn moved away from the fountain to take a photo. The other girls ran around to see it from every direction. Erin edged over to stand by Enrico's side. She leaned over the ledge and peered into the water. "Why are there so many coins in there?" she asked Enrico.

"It is believed that if one throws a coin into the Trevi, one will surely return to Rome." He fished in his pocket and pulled out a small coin. "Here."

He wanted her to come back! How much more proof did she need of his feelings? With a full heart, Erin took the coin and tossed it in the water.

"I've got a surprise for you," Carolyn told the girls at dinner that evening. "We're going to the opera tonight! Enrico knows the stage manager and he was able to get tickets for us."

Trina clapped her hands. "Oh, I've always wanted to go to a real opera!"

"Me too," Sarah agreed. "And it's so perfect to see my first opera in Italy! This is where opera began, isn't it?"

"That's right," Carolyn said.

Erin was pleased, too. She'd never been to an opera either, but her parents went sometimes so she knew that people got very dressed up to go there. Enrico had never seen her all dressed up! She smiled, thinking of how she'd look with her hair in a French braid, wearing the new blue silk dress she'd brought with her . . .

"Oh no!" she wailed. "My clothes! I don't have anything to wear!"

Carolyn looked appropriately sympathetic. "That's right, we still don't have your suitcase. Maybe there's a store still open that we can go to and find a dress for you. I'll check when we get back to the hotel."

"Thanks, Carolyn," Erin said gratefully.

"Will the opera be in Italian?" Megan asked.

"Yes," Carolyn said, "It's *The Marriage of Figaro,* by Mozart. I've been to operas before, and I can usually tell what's going on by watching closely."

"Besides," Erin said, "Enrico can always translate for us."

"Enrico's not going with us," Carolyn told them. "He could only get six tickets."

Erin's heart sank, but she tried not to let it show, even when Katie smirked.

When they arrived back at the pensione, Carolyn said, "We've got two hours before the opera. Erin, I'll check my guidebook and see what stores are open. The rest of you can have a little nap if you like."

But the spark of a daring idea had entered Erin's mind, and she needed to get out of the shopping excursion. "I don't think I need a dress after all, Carolyn. Trina and I wear the same size. Maybe I can borrow something of hers."

"Sure," Trina said, but both she and Carolyn

were looking at her strangely. Erin couldn't blame them. She was usually up for any excuse to go shopping, and Trina's simple, tailored clothes weren't her style at all. But before any of them could comment on this odd behavior, she said, "I'm going to lie down for a little while," and went up to her room.

Megan followed her. "I'm beginning to think you'll never find your suitcase," she said. "I wonder why the other person never called the airport to report hers missing?"

"I don't know," Erin murmured. She was busy thinking through the brilliant plan that was still on her mind.

Megan wandered over to the suitcase and opened it. "Too bad you can't wear this gown," she said, holding up the fancy gold dress. "But I guess it would be too big."

Erin glanced at it. "And too old-fashioned. It looks like something people wore hundreds of years ago." She sat at the dresser and began applying makeup.

"What are you getting ready now for?" Megan asked. "We're not going for two hours."

"I'm going somewhere else first," Erin said.

"Where?"

Erin hesitated. But if she was going to tell anyone, it might as well be Megan. She was romantic enough to understand. "Enrico told me he likes to sit on the Spanish Steps after dinner."

Megan stared at her blankly for a minute. Then she let out an excited gasp. "Are you going to meet him there?"

Erin nodded. "But don't tell, okay? Not even the other girls."

"But we're not supposed to go off by ourselves," Megan reminded her anxiously.

"No one will have to know," Erin assured her. "And I'll be back before we have to leave."

Megan gazed in awe as Erin prepared to leave. "This is so romantic! Sneaking out to meet an older man . . ."

Erin beamed at her. Choosing Megan for a roommate was the best decision she'd ever made. "I'll see you later." She went out, closing the door quietly so no one on the hall would hear. Then she went downstairs and hurried outside.

Thank goodness it was still light out. As she approached the corner of their narrow street, she could see the Spanish Steps looming before her. They seemed to be covered with people. Erin's eyes searched the crowds. She started up the steps, looking in each direction, scanning the faces.

91

Then she caught her breath. There he was, way over on the other side! She started toward him. And then she stopped.

He wasn't alone. Sitting next to him, sitting very close to him, was Carolyn.

Erin crouched down so they couldn't see her. In disbelief, she watched. Enrico's lips moved. Carolyn tossed her head back and laughed. Then, to her horror, Erin saw him lean over and kiss her on the cheek.

She couldn't bear to see any more. Turning, she ran down the stairs. It was amazing that she made it safely to the bottom, her vision was so blurred by tears.

Thank goodness she had her sunglasses with her. As she dragged herself up the stairs in the pensione, she put them on so her puffy eyes wouldn't betray her.

Megan looked up in surprise when Erin walked in. "Why are you back so soon?"

"He wasn't there."

"Oh. I'm going to play cards with Katie and Sarah and Trina. Want to come?"

"No. I'm going to have a nap." She lay down on her bed, her face turned away from Megan. She sensed that Megan was staring at her, but she lay very still and pretended to be sleeping. Finally, Megan left.

Once she was gone, Erin took off the sunglasses and waited for the tears to flow freely. But they didn't come. She didn't feel like crying anymore. All she felt was a burning anger.

So that was why Enrico kept hanging out with them—he wanted to be with Carolyn, not her. The anger churned inside her. Anger at Carolyn and Enrico. Anger at herself for being taken in by his charm. Sooner or later, the other girls would find out that something was going on between Carolyn and Enrico. And Erin would look like a fool. That hurt more than anything else.

Finally, she got up and went into the bathroom. She filled the tub with water, and sat in it for as long as she could stand it. But it didn't make her feel any better.

And when she emerged and remembered that she didn't have any decent clothes to put on, she felt even worse. It was too much to bear. She threw herself back on the bed and cried some more.

The door opened, and Megan came in. Quickly, Erin turned her face away. "Carolyn says we should get ready to leave."

"I'm not going," Erin said.

"Why not?"

"I . . . I have this awful headache." She buried her face in the pillow, and heard Megan walk out. But she returned a moment later. With Carolyn.

"Megan says you're not feeling well."

Erin couldn't bring herself to even look at the counselor. "It's just a headache."

Carolyn reached out to feel her forehead, but Erin brushed the hand away. "I'm okay, really. It's just a fierce headache and I don't want to go out."

"But we can't leave you here alone," Carolyn protested.

Erin eyed her stonily. "I'm not that young, Carolyn. I don't need a baby-sitter."

Carolyn seemed taken aback by her tone. "Erin, something's wrong and it's not just a headache. What's bothering you? Are you upset about your suitcase? We haven't given up trying to find it, you know."

We. She probably meant herself and Enrico. "Nothing's wrong," Erin said through clenched teeth. "I just want to be alone."

Carolyn hesitated. "Well, I suppose it's safe. *Signor* Polloni will be at the reception desk downstairs. It's a shame to waste the ticket, though."

Erin couldn't resist. "You don't have to waste

94

it. You can ask Enrico to go with you. Wouldn't you like that?"

Carolyn's eyes widened. For a moment, she seemed to be at a loss for words. Her hand went to her mouth. "Oh, Erin. I think we need to talk."

"I don't want to talk," Erin said. Her voice was rising. "I just want to be left alone!"

Carolyn sighed. "All right. Come on, Megan." And they left the room.

Erin lay very still. Her eyes drifted to the suitcase in the corner of the room. How could she be upset about that? She could always get a new suitcase, new clothes. But would she ever find someone like Enrico again?

Chapter 8

At lunch the next day, Katie was giggling. "This is wild. Here we are, in Italy, eating lunch at McDonald's!"

Carolyn gazed at them all in amusement. "I guess you all needed a taste of home."

"It's a nice change from pizza and pasta," Trina remarked. Hastily, she turned to Enrico. "No offense, I do love Italian food, too."

"I take no offense at that comment," Enrico replied. "You see, I also love the Big Mac."

Erin dragged a french fry through some ketchup, but left it lying on her plate. She had absolutely no appetite. What a dreary morning it had been. They'd wandered through some old Roman neighborhood, where Enrico had pointed out places of historical interest. Yesterday, Erin would have hung on every word. Today, she couldn't even bring herself to look at him.

No one even seemed to care or notice that she was so miserable. Okay, every now and then she caught Carolyn's concerned eyes on her. But as for the others—they were completely engrossed in themselves. Well, what could she expect from her immature cabin mates? They wouldn't be able to recognize the symptoms of heartbreak.

"I am sorry I wasn't able to join you at the opera last night," Enrico said.

"It was fantastic!" Katie commented.

Megan agreed. "I always thought opera was supposed to be serious. But this one was funny!"

"Even though I couldn't understand what they were singing, I was laughing," Sarah said. She turned to Erin. "It was a crazy story. See, there were all these people, and each one was in love but not with the person they were supposed to be in love with, so they were all sneaking around and hiding and wearing disguises trying to get together with the people they really liked."

Megan looked at Erin and winked. Erin realized she was thinking about the evening before, when Erin sneaked out to find Enrico on the Spanish Steps. Well, if that was what the opera was all about, Erin would call it a tragedy, not a comedy.

"It was a scream," Katie said. "My favorite

character was the guy who worked for the count—what was his name?"

"Cherubino," Trina told her.

Katie explained to Erin. "He was in love with the count's wife. It's too complicated to explain, but he had to disguise himself as a woman to get near the countess."

Trina giggled at the memory. "And this other woman was giving him lessons on how to act feminine."

"I liked that part too," Megan said. "It was weird about that Cherubino guy, though. There was something about him that looked familiar."

"Oh yeah?" Katie grinned. "You know some guys who dress up like women?"

Everyone laughed, except Erin. Enrico turned to her.

"My dear Erin, you do not seem to be yourself today." He paused. "Ah yes, I understand. I have disappointed you."

Erin looked up in horror. Had he seen her on the Spanish Steps last night?

"You see," Enrico said to the others, "I promised to treat Erin to a *gelato*. And I have not yet done so. This afternoon, I will take you all for the best *gelato* in Rome."

How thrilling, Erin thought. *Gelato* would

probably turn out to be something like cala-mari.

As they were leaving McDonald's, Carolyn said, "I have to get a picture of this. Who's going to believe that there's a McDonald's at the foot of the Spanish Steps in the heart of Rome?" She reached in her purse, and groaned. "Darn, I left my camera back at the hotel."

"Oh, but you must have your camera," Enrico said. "This afternoon, we walk along the Appian Way, where you will see many things you will want to photograph."

"Would you guys mind if we go back to the hotel for a moment?" Carolyn asked.

Erin lagged behind the group as they went up the crooked street. To her annoyance, Katie slowed down to walk with her. There was a mischievous glint in her eyes.

"How come you're not walking up there with your boyfriend?"

Erin kept her head high and her mouth shut, trying to make it clear she was in no mood for conversation. But that didn't stop Katie.

"I hate to tell you this, Erin, but I think he's got a thing for Carolyn."

"For your information, I couldn't care less," Erin replied.

Katie stopped teasing. "Hey, are you really upset about that?"

Erin simply gave her a withering look, and marched on ahead. In the Pensione Polloni, the others waited in the lobby while Carolyn went upstairs. Erin went up to her room too. She didn't need anything, but at least she could have a few minutes away from the group.

She flung herself on her bed. Megan's program from the opera was lying on the floor next to it. Listlessly, she picked it up and flipped through it.

Inside, there were photographs of the stars in their costumes. Erin scanned them without much interest. And then, one photo seemed to leap off the page and hit her in the eye. It was the man who was dressed as a woman. And Megan was right. Something about him looked very familiar.

She leaped off the bed and opened the mysterious suitcase. Then she almost exclaimed out loud. Yes—it was the very same dress as the one in the photo!

She snatched up the program and turned to the cast list. What did the girls say the character's name was? Cherry something . . . and there it was. Cherubino. Played by Carlo Bellini.

No wonder Enrico had never been able to locate the owner of the suitcase. He was calling every Bellini and asking for *signora* or *signorina*. But the C. Bellini who owned the suitcase was a *signor*.

She was on the verge of racing downstairs to tell the others. Then she stopped herself. They didn't care about her. She wasn't about to ask for their help.

Quickly, she examined the program. It announced the performance dates, and there was a matinee that very afternoon.

In the hallway, she heard Carolyn's door close, and then her footsteps. They were all down in the lobby. How could she get out of the hotel without being seen?

She remembered seeing a door in the breakfast room leading out to the back of the hotel. She left the room and tiptoed down the stairs. She could see them in the lobby, but no one was watching the stairs. Edging around a tall fern, she managed to get into the breakfast room without being seen. Then she hurried out the door.

She ran down a back alley to the closest piazza. There, she hailed a taxi. "The Opera," she told the driver.

It was farther away than she thought it would be. By the time she arrived, it was only a few minutes before the matinee. Breathlessly, she ran up to the box office, and prayed that the ticket seller spoke English.

"One ticket," she said, fumbling in her purse for her wallet. But the man shook his head. "No tickets. Sold out."

For a moment, she panicked. Then she had another idea. She ran out of the building and around to the side of it. She knew there must be some sort of stage door, where the actors went in and out. And she found it. But it was locked. She knocked, as hard as she could, but no one came.

She leaned against the wall. Now what? She'd just have to wait until the opera was over and the performers came out. But what was she going to do in the meantime?

She began wandering around the area. Roaming through shops, she glanced at items without even seeing them. She went into an art gallery, and moved from painting to painting. Leaving, she couldn't even remember what kind of paintings they were.

She glanced at her watch. There was still lots of time to kill. Across the street, she saw a group of girls, probably about her age. They were walking arm in arm, laughing and chattering loudly in Italian.

A lonely feeling swept over her. That's where she should be, she thought—with her friends, enjoying herself. Camp Spaghetti, Megan had called this trip. It didn't feel much like camp to her.

This was supposed to be a holiday, and what was she doing? Chasing after an opera singer who just might have her suitcase. And sulking because a boy wasn't in love with her.

No, not a boy. A man. A man who was charming and affectionate and who spoke in a romantic way. Well, how else was he supposed to speak? After all, he *was* a Roman. It was Erin who had tried to make it mean something special. It was her own foolishness that made her want to believe it meant love.

She stopped at a newspaper stand and bought a magazine. Taking it into a coffee shop, she ordered a soda and leafed through the pages. It was all in Italian, but that didn't matter. She wasn't in the mood to read anyway.

She kept checking her watch. Finally, she decided it was time to get back. Returning to the opera house, she saw the audience emerging. She hurried over to the side, and stationed herself just by the stage door.

It dawned on her that she might not even recognize this Carlo Bellini. In the picture, he'd been disguised as a woman—but he wouldn't be leaving the theater looking like that.

She held her breath as a man came out the stage door. *"Signor* Bellini?" she called. The man glanced at her curiously, but kept on walking. She ignored the couple of women who emerged next, but they were followed by a group of men.

"Signor Bellini?"

One of them turned and said something to her in Italian. He kept on going, before Erin could ask him if he spoke English.

More women came out. And then another man. *Signor* Bellini?" Erin tried again.

The man didn't say anything. But he cocked his thumb toward the door, as if to say that *Signor* Bellini was still inside.

When the door opened again, a woman was coming out. Erin slid past her and went inside. *"Signor* Bellini?" she called.

An older, kindly-looking man appeared. "No, no, *signorina."* He spoke in Italian.

"Please, I don't speak Italian," Erin cried. "Can you speak English?"

He just kept shaking his head, saying "no, no." He took her arm, and led her back to the door. He thinks I'm just a fan, Erin thought wildly.

Gently, the older man pushed her outside and began to close the door. Erin struggled to keep it open. "Please! I have to see *Signor* Bellini!"

The man's face became firm. Just then, the man looked over her shoulder and squinted. "Enrico!" This was followed by a string of Italian.

Erin whirled around. There was Enrico, running toward them. In one hand, he carried the suitcase from Erin's room. He put the other arm around Erin, and spoke in Italian to the man. The man's expression underwent a dramatic change. A second later, he was ushering both Erin and Enrico back inside.

He made a gesture which seemed to indicate they should wait there. Enrico turned to Erin, and for once, he wasn't smiling. "Ah, Erin. You have everyone most frightened at the hotel! We have been looking everywhere for you!"

While his tone wasn't exactly angry, it was definitely stern. In fact, he sounded quite a bit like Erin's father when he was annoyed with her.

Suddenly, Erin felt very sheepish. "I'm sorry."

"You should be sorry," Enrico said. "Carolyn is in great distress, and your friends are frightened. We have searched the area for you."

"How did you figure out I was here?"

"Little Megan. She remembered why the character in the opera was familiar to her. It was the dress he wore, the same as in this suitcase. We looked in the opera program and saw the name Bellini."

The stage manager returned, accompanied by a young, handsome man. "*Signor* Bellini?" Enrico asked.

As the man nodded, he spotted the suitcase in Enrico's hand. He let out an exclamation. The two men spoke in Italian, and then the opera singer hurried away. When he came back, he had Erin's suitcase in his hand.

Enrico explained to Erin. "The opera company was performing in the United States. On the last night of performance, *Signor* Bellini was late in returning his costume and other things, and he had to take them back to Rome himself."

"And I picked up his suitcase by mistake," Erin finished.

"That is correct. Fortunately, the opera has duplicates of the wardrobe."

Signor Bellini opened the suitcase he carried. Erin let out a huge sigh of relief. "Yes, it's mine. Could you tell him how sorry I am?"

Enrico relayed her message in Italian. *Signor*

Bellini responded with a smile, and Enrico translated. "He says he was also at fault, for not putting any identification on his suitcase."

The suitcases were exchanged. The three of them left the theater together. When they reached the street, Enrico waved to a taxi. As the taxi approached, *Signor* Bellini shook hands with him. Erin put out her hand too. But *Signor* Bellini didn't shake it. Instead, he leaned down, and kissed her lightly on both cheeks. He said something in Italian to Enrico, and then, with a wave, he walked away.

Erin touched her cheeks in wonderment as she and Enrico got into the taxi. "What did he just say to you?"

"He said you are a beautiful young lady. And that he would like to meet you again, in about ten years."

"Ten years," Erin repeated. She sighed deeply. That was a long, long time.

Enrico smiled, and patted her hand. "Perhaps, only eight."

Chapter 9

As the taxi approached the Pensione Polloni, a sense of dread filled Erin. Carolyn would be in there, absolutely furious at her. Maybe she'd even called Erin's parents back home.

And the girls—they'd be pretty mad too. She'd ruined their day. Maybe even their whole holiday. If Carolyn had called Erin's parents, they might all be on the next flight home.

She hesitated outside the hotel while Enrico paid the taxi driver. Above her, the sky was gray and cloudy, which perfectly matched her mood. Maybe she wouldn't care if they all had to go home today. Maybe she *wanted* to go home. With her friends all angry with her, and no romance, what was the point of staying?

Enrico took her firmly by the arm and led her inside. She could see them all, waiting for her

108

in the lobby. And she steeled herself for the on-slaught of anger.

What she actually encountered was totally unexpected. The moment they saw her, Carolyn rushed at her with open arms and held her tightly. "Oh, Erin! Thank goodness, you're all right!"

She was joined by the others, and they all seemed to be trying to hug Erin at once. Megan was actually crying. To her embarrassment, Erin felt tears trickling down her own face.

"I'm sorry," she said, over and over. "I'm really, really, sorry."

Carolyn took the suitcase from Enrico. "Let's take this up to your room. Girls, wait here."

Erin followed her up the stairs. Once they were inside the room, Carolyn sat down on the bed. "Erin . . ."

Erin swallowed. Now the lecture would begin. "Yes?"

"I think I'm the one who should apologize to you."

Erin looked at her in surprise. "What for?"

"I should have been more sensitive to your feelings. I should have tried to talk to you about it."

"About what? My suitcase?"

"No. About Enrico." She took Erin's hand in

hers. "Katie told me how you felt about him. Now, don't get mad at her. We were all frantic when we couldn't find you. I thought you had run away! I begged the girls to give me some sort of clue, some idea why you would do that." She hesitated before continuing. "Then Megan told me you went to the Spanish Steps yesterday after dinner. You saw me there with Enrico, didn't you?"

Erin nodded, but she couldn't look Carolyn in the face. "I hope you'll both be very happy."

"Oh, Erin! We're just becoming friends, Enrico and I! But even if a romance did develop . . . well, you can't feel that we're in competition. I'm twenty years old, Erin, and so is Enrico. You're twelve. I know you're very mature for your age. But there's still a big difference between twelve and twenty. Can you see that?"

Slowly, Erin nodded again. Carolyn's words didn't insult her, or upset her. Somewhere, in the back of her mind, she must have always known that what Carolyn was saying was true. "I guess . . . I guess I just wanted something romantic to happen to me here."

"And maybe something will," Carolyn said warmly. "But with someone your own age, or a little bit older. Not with a twenty-year-old man. It just couldn't work out."

Erin tried to imagine how she would have felt if Enrico had been more romantic. She pictured him kissing her, on the lips. For some reason, the feeling she got wasn't romantic at all. It was sort of . . . scary.

"Yeah," she said finally. "I guess you're right."

"Next time you have feelings like this, Erin, talk to me, okay? I won't laugh at you. I was twelve once, you know. Remind me sometime to tell you about the time, when I was your age, and I had this incredible crush on my older brother's best friend."

"What happened?" Erin asked.

Carolyn grinned. "I'll tell you later. Right now, everyone's waiting for us downstairs. And we have to take Enrico up on his promise to buy us all *gelatos.*"

Erin eyed her suitcase. "Can I have a minute to change my clothes?"

"Absolutely," Carolyn said. "See you in a few minutes."

Erin rummaged through her suitcase. It was wonderful seeing all the cute things she'd brought again. She changed into some leggings and a long sweater, and went downstairs.

For a moment, she thought they'd all gone

and left her. Then, from behind her, she heard a voice. "You are Erin?"

She turned. A boy stood there.

"Yes, I'm Erin."

"My name is Antonio Polloni. I am the brother of Enrico."

Erin tried not to gape. He looked like a younger version of Enrico—a little shorter, but with the same curly black hair and dark flashing eyes. "How do you do?" she managed.

"I do fine," he replied. "And you do fine also, I hope?"

Erin stifled a giggle. "Yes, I do fine. Where is everyone?"

"They wait for us outside. Shall we go?"

Never before had Erin seen a boy her own age with such manners. He took her arm and held the door open.

When the others saw them, they started up the street. "The very good place for *gelato* is just around this corner," Antonio said. "You like *gelato?*"

With Antonio, Erin felt like she could be honest. "I've never had *gelato* before."

He seemed astonished to hear that. "But that is impossible! It is my understanding that *gelato* is very popular in the United States of America!"

Erin was about to say, "Not in Pennsylvania," when Antonio steered her into a little shop. The other cabin six girls were already *ooh*ing and *ahh*ing around a glass case. Erin moved in closer to see what was stirring all this enthusiasm.

"Ice cream!" she exclaimed.

"Yes, that is the word you use," Antonio said. "Ice cream. You have eaten this before?"

"Oh, sure, lots of times." Then, quickly she added, "But you have some different flavors here. Could you recommend one for me?"

He seemed pleased to do that. They all got their ice creams, and went to sit at tables outside. Miraculously, the clouds had disappeared, the sun was out, and the sky was blue.

Megan licked at her *gelato.* "Mmm. My father said Italian ice cream was the best in the world. I think he's right."

Erin agreed. Of course, she wasn't sure if it was the *gelato* or the beautiful weather or Antonio. Or maybe it was just being with her friends. But Rome suddenly seemed like the best possible place to be.

Katie raised her cone in the air. "I want to propose a toast. Here's to Camp Spaghetti!"

While the others laughed, Antonio turned to Erin. "What does this mean, Camp Spaghetti?"

113

"It's kind of a long story," Erin said.

Antonio smiled. "Perhaps later we can take a long walk. And you can tell me all about this Camp Spaghetti."

Erin smiled back. That sounded like a very nice idea to her.

"Why haven't I met you before today?" she asked.

"My brother has wanted me to meet you," Antonio said. "He said you are enchanting. And very mature. I was a . . . how would you say? A coward? I was afraid you would think I am too young for you."

"How old are you?" Erin asked.

"Thirteen. Do you think that is too young?"

"Oh, no." Erin tossed her hair, tilted her face, and gave him her best sidelong look. "I think that's exactly right."

MEET THE GIRLS FROM CABIN SIX IN

(#16) HAPPILY EVER AFTER	76555-1 ($3.50 US/$4.25 Can)
(#15) CHRISTMAS BREAK	76553-5 ($2.99 US/$3.50 Can)
(#14) MEGAN'S GHOST	76552-7 ($2.99 US/$3.50 Can)
(#13) BIG SISTER BLUES	76551-9 ($2.95 US/$3.50 Can)
(#12) THE TENNIS TRAP	76184-X ($2.95 US/$3.50 Can)
(#11) THE PROBLEM WITH PARENTS	
	76183-1 ($2.95 US/$3.50 Can)
(#10) ERIN AND THE MOVIE STAR	76181-5 ($2.95 US/$3.50 Can)
(#9) THE NEW-AND-IMPROVED SARAH	
	76180-7 ($2.95 US/$3.50 Can)
(#8) TOO MANY COUNSELORS	75913-6 ($2.95 US/$3.50 Can)
(#7) A WITCH IN CABIN SIX	75912-8 ($2.95 US/$3.50 Can)
(#6) KATIE STEALS THE SHOW	75910-1 ($2.95 US/$3.50 Can)
(#5) LOOKING FOR TROUBLE	75909-8 ($2.95 US/$3.50 Can)
(#4) NEW GIRL IN CABIN SIX	75703-6 ($2.95 US/$3.50 Can)
(#3) COLOR WAR!	75702-8 ($3.50 US/$4.25 Can)
(#2) CABIN SIX PLAYS CUPID	75701-X ($2.95 US/$3.50 Can)
(#1) NO BOYS ALLOWED!	75700-1 ($2.95 US/$3.50 Can)

Celebrating 40 Years of Cleary Kids!

CAMELOT presents
CLEARY FAVORITES!

☐ **HENRY HUGGINS**
70912-0 ($3.50 US/$4.25 Can)

☐ **HENRY AND BEEZUS**
70914-7 ($3.50 US/$4.25 Can)

☐ **HENRY AND THE CLUBHOUSE**
70915-5 ($3.50 US/$4.25 Can)

☐ **ELLEN TEBBITS**
70913-9 ($3.50 US/$4.25 Can)

☐ **HENRY AND RIBSY**
70917-1 ($3.50 US/$4.25 Can)

☐ **BEEZUS AND RAMONA**
70918-X ($3.50 US/$4.25 Can)

☐ **RAMONA AND HER FATHER**
70916-3 ($3.50 US/$4.25 Can)

☐ **MITCH AND AMY**
70925-2 ($3.50 US/$4.25 Can)

☐ **RUNAWAY RALPH**
70953-8 ($3.50 US/$4.25 Can)

☐ **HENRY AND THE PAPER ROUTE**
70921-X ($3.50 US/$4.25 Can)

☐ **RAMONA AND HER MOTHER**
70952-X ($3.50 US/$4.25 Can)

☐ **OTIS SPOFFORD**
70919-8 ($3.50 US/$4.25 Can)

☐ **THE MOUSE AND THE MOTORCYCLE**
70924-4 ($3.50 US/$4.25 Can)

☐ **SOCKS**
70926-0 ($3.50 US/$4.25 Can)

☐ **EMILY'S RUNAWAY IMAGINATION**
70923-6 ($3.50 US/$4.25 Can)

☐ **MUGGIE MAGGIE**
71087-0 ($3.50 US/$4.25 Can)

From Out of the Shadows...
Stories Filled With Mystery
and Suspense by
MARY DOWNING HAHN

THE TIME OF THE WITCH
71116-8/$2.99 US/$3.50 Can

It is the middle of the night and suddenly Laura is awake, trembling with fear. Just beneath her bedroom window, a strange-looking old woman is standing in the moonlight. A big black crow is perched on her shoulder and she is looking up—staring back at Laura.

THE DEAD MAN IN INDIAN CREEK
71362-4/$2.95 US/$3.50 Can

THE DOLL IN THE GARDEN
70865-5/$3.50 US/$4.25 Can

FOLLOWING THE MYSTERY MAN
70677-6/$2.95 US/$3.50 Can

TALLAHASSEE HIGGINS
70500-1/$3.50 US/$4.25 Can

WAIT TILL HELEN COMES
70442-0/$3.50 US/$4.25 Can